Praise for T

'A spine-tingling reac

\ rollicking ghoulish horror story written with
.reat pace and historical detail. Children will love
i.' *Daily Mail*

npressive . . . a rollicking historical yarn about
eetwise boys foiling a dastardly conspiracy.'
ily Telegraph

u can always trust Justin Richards to provide a
)-roaring story that will keep you on the edge of
your seat from start to finish, and this follow-up to
The Death Collector is no exception . . . This is the
kind of book for reading late at night under the
covers. A perfect Halloween read for anyone who
prefers an adventure over gore.' *Waterstone's Books Quarterly*

Praise for *The Death Collector*:

'This is a real page-turner. The book starts with a
dead man walking back into his kitchen and then

dragging his terrified dog out for a walk! . . . Once you've finished it, you'll want to find another book just as exciting.' CBBC Newsround

'A very exciting novel, reminiscent in some ways of Philip Pullman's Victorian novels . . . a real page-turner – and the ending is quite spectacular.' *Books for Keeps*

'A thoroughly enjoyable romp full of chases, high drama and a hint of romance in great old-fashioned style. Simply smashing.' *Kirkus Reviews*

Praise for *The Chaos Code*:

'*The Chaos Code* is a globetrotting tour de force in the mould of *The Da Vinci Code*, but better written.' *Write Away*

'Exciting . . . thought-provoking.' *Daily Mail*

JUSTIN RICHARDS

faber and faber

First published in 2010
by Faber and Faber Limited
Bloomsbury House
74–7 Great Russell Street
London WC1B 3DA

Typeset by Faber and Faber Limited
Printed in England by Bookmarque, Croydon, UK

A CIP record for this book
is available from the British Library

ISBN 978–0–571–24508–6

THE SCHOOL OF NIGHT

SEARCH

In the fifteenth century, an alchemist called Gabriel Diablo sought to summon a mighty demon: Mortagula. He thought that if he could control the demon he would be the most powerful man on earth.

But the agents of the Memento Mori stopped him and took away the five Artefacts that he needed to summon the demon:

- a Dagger to control Mortagula.
- an Amulet which could open a Gateway to Hell and allow the demons to enter our world.
- a Crystal that focuses energy to control or harness the forces of darkness.
- The Book of Darkness Rising – Diablo's own notes on how he planned to summon the demon.
- The Book of Lost Souls – an ancient book of instructions for controlling demons and the dead.

In 1729, the Pope dissolved the Memento Mori and its surviving members went into hiding. What happened to the Artefacts remains a mystery.

If anyone gathered together the five Artefacts, they would have the power to summon forth the demon Mortagula – to control or to destroy the world.

Luckily, the Artefacts have remained lost and hidden . . . until now.

PREV 1 2 3 4 5 6 7 ... NEXT

DEMON STORM

1

A WOMAN WHO DROWNED HERSELF OVER sixty years ago stood by the lake watching Sam. The dead woman's hair was matted with pondweed, and her plain white dress was stained and torn. Her eyes were sunken black in her pale face. Water dripped from her outstretched, pleading arms – dripped and fell and never landed on the muddy ground . . .

'What are you looking at?' Ben asked.

'Nothing,' Sam said. 'Nothing and no one. It's not important.'

The woman slowly lowered her arms. She gave the faintest shake of her head, then turned and walked sadly away. Back into the lake. There were no ripples as the water closed over her head – just as it had sixty-three years ago.

'You're always looking at nothing,' Ben grumbled. 'Why can't I see it too?'

'Be quiet, Ben,' Sam told her brother, though

she spoke gently. 'We're here to make a promise, remember?'

She took her young brother's hand, hoping he would think she was trembling from the cold. Together they walked down to the side of the lake. There was a narrow path – barely more than a muddy track – running along the shore. When they last came here, exactly a year ago on Ben's twelfth birthday, the track had been hard and dry. Now it was damp and slippery, mud squelching and oozing beneath their shoes.

They could see the house from the corner where the path bent almost back on itself to follow the water. A dark silhouette against the gathering clouds and the grey of the evening. The broken windows were empty sockets, the boarded-up door a gaping mouth.

'We really used to live there?' Ben wasn't impressed.

'A long time ago.'

'With our mum and dad?'

Sam looked away, pulling Ben after her as they left the house behind. 'With our mum and dad.'

'I don't remember Mum and Dad. I remember the MacPhersons. Mr MacPherson was in the army. We had to leave. They were nice.'

'Yes. And before the MacPhersons we were with the Bakers. And before that the Neales.'

'Did we have to leave them too?'

Sam didn't answer. The MacPhersons had been understanding, the first few times. But Sam had screamed at the ghosts too often. She'd refused to go in the room where the old man rocked himself to sleep in a chair that wasn't there. She saw the men Captain MacPherson had killed in the Gulf, following him everywhere he went . . .

The Bakers hadn't even tried. The first time she went pale and started to shake at the sight of what hung from the gibbet on Gallows Hill they'd sent Sam and Ben back. And as for the Neales . . .

A wooden jetty stuck out into the lake. The planks were rotted and broken. A frayed rope hung from a splintered mooring post. The faintest impression of young James Anguin, who'd fallen out of his fishing boat and never been seen again, nodded to Sam. She nodded back. He was always there. Always would be.

'Here we are,' Sam said.

'Let's go out on the jetty.'

'Best not. The wood's pretty rotten. It's not safe.'

'I did last year.'

'It was the year before. You're much bigger and

heavier now, and the wood's even more rotten and weak.'

'We'll do it here, then,' Ben decided, standing stiffly on the path at the edge of the jetty.

'Here,' Sam agreed.

She took her brother's hands between her own and looked down at him. Ben's dark hair was blowing round his face in the breeze. Her own long, dark hair was whipped into a frenzy, but she kept hold of Ben's hands as they promised.

They made the same promise every year. Even now, neither of them could be sure they wouldn't be separated from each other. When they were younger, it was a constant worry. Every year they were able to stay together was a bonus. The only constant in their lives was each other. Every year they were thankful for that. Every year they promised each other they'd stay together. They'd never be split up.

'You first,' Ben said.

'I, Samantha Foundling – or whatever my real name is – do promise here at the lake, close to the house that was our last proper home, to look after my brother, Ben Foundling.'

'Or whatever his name is,' Ben said, giggling.

They'd had so many names, so many different

families. Neither of them really remembered their own surname any more. Maybe it really was Foundling.

'I promise I'll always be there for you, no matter what,' Sam went on. 'I promise that nothing will ever take me away from you. Not ever.' She forced a smile. 'There. Now it's your turn.'

Ben nodded. 'I promise too. All that stuff. Together forever, no matter what. And we'll come here every year, like we always have, to make our promise, won't we?'

'We will. Every year. Without fail.'

Ben pulled his hands away and enfolded his big sister in a hug. 'I love you, Sam.'

'I love you too, Ben.'

They stood silent and still, holding on tight, for several minutes. The darkness closed in around them, and the late James Anguin faded with the last of the October light.

Finally, Sam gently pulled away. 'We'd better be getting back.'

The MacPhersons had tried, Sam knew that. Just as she knew how difficult she must be to live with. Better now, but two years ago, when she was not much older than Ben was now . . . She didn't blame them. Over a year of a thirteen-year-old's screaming and temper and panic and tears . . .

She could control it better these days. She could ignore the things she saw – make a point of not looking at them. Some, like James Anguin, just watched her. They just *were*. But others, she knew, meant her harm.

Only Ben knew that she could see things – or 'nothing', as they pretended. But even he didn't really understand. He was just thirteen – how could he understand? She couldn't when she was that age. She was nearly fifteen now and she still couldn't understand it. Why was she different? Was it because of something that had happened? Something at the house by the lake when they had parents and names of their own? There was something on the very edge of her memory . . . Perhaps that was why she was drawn back to this exact same place every year to make her promise to her brother.

'Will we be in trouble for going out?' Ben asked.

They were sitting on the bus. Sam stared straight ahead, not looking at the woman opposite who clutched a new bag from a shop that had closed a decade ago.

'I doubt anyone has even noticed we've gone,' she told him. 'We'll be back before bedtime.'

The boys and the girls had separate dormitories. Ben's was divided into cubicles with a curtain across the front of each. The older girls were in shared rooms, two or three in each. Except Sam – she had a bedroom to herself. No one would share with her. They all knew she had such nightmares.

The bus turned sharply at a T-junction. Sam glanced out of the window. The grey lady was leaning out of the window of the old house on the corner of Renfrew Avenue. She was screaming. Sam looked away.

The closest bus stop to the home was a good ten minutes' walk away. It was dark now. The street lights cast a sickly orange glow through the evening. The iron gates were dark silhouettes behind which the driveway led up to the Victorian building. There was a newer block stuck on the side, which housed the girls' rooms. It had been built in the 1960s, with no thought that it should complement the main house – pale, square, flat-roofed.

They all called it *the home*, though as it provided not just somewhere to live but also their education it was more like a small boarding school. Except that there were never any school holidays, never any real homes to go back to when term ended . . .

At least Sam's room was in the new block, where

there were fewer ghosts. The old house was full of them – ghosts and memories and a gargoyle at the top of a downpipe round the back that watched Sam through sightless stone eyes.

They walked up the drive, hand in hand. The lights in the new block shone bright, but the shuttered windows of the old house were dark and empty.

'What happens when you're sixteen?' Ben asked, his voice trembling. It was something he'd thought about a lot, but he hadn't dared to ask before. 'People can leave the home when they're sixteen.'

'I won't leave you,' she repeated. 'I just promised, didn't I? And when I'm old enough – maybe when I'm sixteen or eighteen, or whenever I'm allowed – then I'll take you with me. We'll find somewhere else, just the two of us.'

'Will we be a family?'

'Yes,' Sam told him, squeezing his hand. 'We'll be a family. Nothing will stop that. Things will be so different just a year from now.'

2

'JUST A YEAR,' SAM HAD SAID. BUT TO BEN A YEAR seemed a very long time.

Even so, the days became weeks and the weeks became months. Ben saw less of Sam. She was studying for her GCSEs. Whenever she could, though, she spent time with Ben. They would walk in the grounds or, better still, go down into the town.

But they never went to the lake. That was a special place, reserved for the promise meeting. Waiting for them to return on Ben's birthday.

And because a year had seemed such a long time, Ben was surprised how soon it passed. How soon his birthday approached again . . .

'It's only two weeks until your birthday,' Sam said as they returned late from a stolen walk.

They weren't supposed to be out together and already it was getting dark. Ben was going slowly, taking as long as he could to walk back to the home.

The lights of a car swung across the gravel drive as it turned in at the gate behind them. Sam pulled Ben to one side to let the car go by. It gave a brief toot of acknowledgement as it passed. It looked like an old car – classic rather than vintage. It parked outside the home. By the time they reached the front door, there was no sign of the driver.

Two of the bulbs in the main chandelier had gone. The entrance hall was a criss-cross of shadows and light. A figure stood in the darkness by the stairs to the boys' dormitory. His face was in darkness.

'Samantha?'

He stepped into the light and Ben saw that it was Mr Magill. Ben liked Mr Magill – he was friendly and fair. He always wore a tie, and he made jokes while he was teaching the younger boys maths. On Fridays he gave them lollipops.

'We just went for a walk,' Sam said quickly. 'Round the grounds, that's all. Didn't notice the time.'

Mr Magill raised his eyebrows. 'Or that it had got dark? You're a senior, so you're allowed out. But Ben's only a junior.'

'I'm thirteen,' Ben told him. 'And it's my birthday in two weeks.'

'Really?' He smiled at them – a real smile. 'But even so . . . As long as it was just round the grounds,' he said, in a voice that made it clear he knew it wasn't. 'Now, be quick and hang your coats up. There's a special assembly in the main hall in ten minutes, so it's lucky you got back in time.'

'What's the assembly for?' Ben wondered.

'If you wait ten minutes I expect you'll find out. Make sure you're there.' He was looking at Sam as he spoke.

There was a large walk-in cupboard under the main stairs where the children kept their coats and outdoor shoes. By the time Ben and Sam had hung their coats up and put on their indoor slippers, some of the other boys were coming down the main staircase from their dormitory or the social room.

Miss Haining was with them. She was a sour-faced middle-aged woman who taught literacy, as thin as a street lamp. Her long fingers were like gnarled sticks and she pointed one of them crookedly at Sam.

'You, girl!' She called everyone either 'boy' or 'girl' despite knowing all their names. 'What are you doing here, girl?'

'I'm going to the assembly, like everyone else.'

'And where have you been? You know you're not

allowed in the boys' dormitories and social rooms.'

'This is the hall,' Sam said coldly. 'I haven't been anywhere. Certainly not up in the boys' dormitories or social rooms.'

'Then what are you doing here? Your room's in the new block.'

'She came to meet me,' Ben said. 'So we can go to the assembly together.'

Miss Haining stared at Ben through flint-cold eyes. 'I didn't ask you, boy.' She turned back to Sam. 'I haven't seen you since lunch.'

'I haven't seen you either,' Sam said.

'Where have you been?'

'I was reading. Where were you?'

Miss Haining seemed to swell up as she drew a deep breath. Finally she said, 'Don't let me catch you somewhere you shouldn't be again.'

'You didn't catch me this time,' Sam muttered, making Ben grin.

His sister's irritation didn't last. 'Come on. Let's go or we'll be late.' She smiled and took Ben's hand. He was tempted to pull it away. He was too old to hold hands. But he knew it wasn't really that Sam wanted to hold his hand. She wanted him to hold *her* hand. To keep her safe from the 'nothing' she saw all around them.

They followed the other children along the corridor to the main hall. Sam looked neither left nor right. She gripped Ben's hand so hard it made his eyes water. But he didn't tell her. It was bad here in the old Victorian mansion. Steeped in memories and echoes of the past, it had been a house, a school, even a mental hospital. They all left their impression – impressions that you could almost feel.

Impressions that Ben knew his sister could *see*.

The main hall had once been the dining room. It was a large, rectangular room, its ceiling criss-crossed with dark wooden beams. The windows were set high in the walls – arched and framed with pale stone. Double doors opened into one end of the room and at the other end there was a small gallery looking down into the hall. There was another, smaller doorway beneath the gallery.

A narrow staircase led up to the gallery from the corridor that ran behind the hall. The door was kept bolted and the children were forbidden to go up there, because the floor wasn't safe. But of course they did.

Ben and Sam were among the last of the children to arrive. There weren't that many children at the home, but the hall was crowded when they were all together. Mr Magill had everyone lining up between the long, narrow tables where they ate their meals.

'Any order, it doesn't matter. And it won't take long, so let's keep it quiet and sensible, shall we?'

Miss Haining was watching through narrowed eyes. Mr Casswell, the history teacher, was talking quietly with her. Ben picked up some of their conversation as he and Sam walked past to join the line-up.

'I don't recall such a thing happening before,' Mr Casswell was saying.

'Mental aptitude inspection,' she muttered back. 'As if you can tell just by looking at them if the children are in sound mind or need special treatment.'

'Well, he is an expert, apparently . . .'

Ben glanced at Sam, but she was still looking straight ahead. They stood between little Chris Summers and Jaz Amrij.

'What's going on?' Jaz asked Sam. 'Identity parade, is it – someone been shoplifting again?'

Sam shrugged. 'Dunno. Some sort of inspection.'

'They going to look in our ears or check for nits or something?' Chris wondered.

There was silence as the door under the gallery opened and a man stepped into the room. He was tall and broad, dressed in a dark suit and a plain white shirt with a navy-blue tie. His black hair was cut short, so he looked like a businessman. Or an off-duty soldier. He was carrying a wooden box.

Behind the man was a young girl – younger than Ben, perhaps ten or eleven years old. She was pale and thin, with her mouse-brown hair tied back in a ponytail. Her eyes were wide and were constantly moving, looking at everyone and everything, darting back and forth. She was wearing a pair of charcoal-grey trousers and a white blouse with a plain blazer over it. Maybe it was her school uniform, but there was no insignia or design on the blazer.

The man put the wooden box down on the dining table opposite where the children had lined up. The top was rounded and there were metal handles fixed to each end. It looked more like a small trunk, or a pirate's treasure chest. Metal bands were braced round the wood and there was a large keyhole set in the front.

The man's voice was strong and deep, echoing

in the large room. 'You may ask your colleagues to leave now, Mr Magill. I'm sure we can cope between us.'

Ben grinned at Miss Haining's expression as she stamped from the room. Mr Casswell raised his eyebrows at Mr Magill, who spread his hands as if to say it was nothing to do with him. Mr Magill followed Miss Haining and Mr Casswell to the door, then closed it firmly behind them.

'Thank you all for coming. This won't take long,' Mr Magill announced, turning back to face the line of children. 'And it's absolutely nothing to worry about. No one's in trouble or anything.'

The man with the box was standing looking at them, his hands thrust deep in his jacket pockets. After a short pause he spoke. 'As Mr Magill says, this will only take a few moments. I shall probably ask one or two of you to stay behind for a few words, but the rest of you – as soon as I tap you on the shoulder, you can go.'

He started at the end of the line furthest from Ben and Sam. Bradley Mulverton was the first and he stared back at the man sullenly. The man turned to glance at the mousy-haired girl, who was now sitting on the table beside the wooden box. She was swinging her legs and now shook her head.

The man tapped Bradley on the shoulder. 'You may go.'

It was different with Megan Philps, who was next in line. The man seemed hardly to look at her. He had taken a mobile phone from his pocket. It was the sort that folded shut and he flipped it open, holding it up in front of Megan and staring at the screen.

'Yes, please, if you would stay behind for now.'

'Can I sit down?'

The man ignored her, but Mr Magill told her she could wait on the bench beside the other dining table. Soon a couple more children had joined her. The man passed slowly along the line, still glancing at his phone every now and again – occasionally staring at it for a while before deciding whether to keep someone behind or let them go.

Sometimes he turned to the girl, who either nodded or shook her head to give her opinion. The man always did what she suggested – if she nodded they stayed, if she shook her head they could go.

Finally, the man reached Chris, who was standing next to Sam. Ben could see that the man's face seemed lined with sorrow and dark determination. He glanced at the phone and Ben leaned out of line to try to see what he was looking at. But the man lowered the phone again. Was he getting texts or checking his email or something?

'You can go,' the man told Chris.

'Thank you, sir,' Chris mumbled. 'See you,' he said to Sam and Ben and Jaz, before hurrying over to where Mr Magill opened the door for him.

The man stepped across to look at Sam. He glanced at her and began to raise his phone. Then he hesitated and frowned.

'Have we met before?' he asked.

Sam shook her head. 'Don't think so.'

'Maybe at another home or school?'

'I'd remember,' she told him.

The man clicked his tongue, but did not reply. He raised the phone and held it in front of Sam. His frown deepened. He turned to look at the girl sitting on the table behind.

She was also frowning, her mouth slightly open as if surprised. Staring at Sam.

'Gemma?' the man prompted.

She swallowed and nodded quickly. 'Yes.' Her voice was quiet and nervous. 'Definitely yes.'

'Please wait with the others,' the man told Sam.

He barely glanced at Ben, didn't even bother to check his phone. 'You can go,' he said. 'And so can you,' he told Jaz.

'Why are you keeping them here?' Ben demanded. His voice was shaking, but he had to know what was going to happen to Sam.

The man turned away without answering. Mr Magill patted Ben on the shoulder.

'Come on. Time to go. Sam will be OK. It's nothing to worry about. Just a quick test. And I know how much you hate tests. Both of you,' he added, leading Ben and Jaz to the door. 'It's nearly time to go up for bed. You'll see Sam in the morning and she can tell you all about it then. OK?'

'OK,' Ben agreed sulkily. But it wasn't OK. And he wasn't going to bed until he knew what was happening.

The bolt had already been drawn back. Maybe someone had left the door unbolted by accident. Or maybe, Ben realised, someone was already up on the gallery, watching what was happening in the main hall.

He couldn't think who it might be – unless Jaz or one of the other kids was as curious as he was about what was going on. Just in case, Ben took the steps carefully and slowly. He kept close to the wall, knowing from experience that this meant the old wooden stairs were less likely to creak.

He paused almost at the top and peered round the corner, across the dimly lit gallery.

A dark shape stood at the other end – stick-thin arms outstretched as she held the gallery rail. Her nose was a distinctive blade of shadow. Miss Haining.

For a moment, Ben wondered if he should creep back down the stairs. But only for a moment.

There was a table along the gallery. A long, narrow table used by the decorators who had finished and left months ago. They'd also left rolls of lining paper and a pot of dried-up paint with a brush stuck into it. You could pick up the whole pot by the brush handle.

The table cast an even darker shadow across the gloom. Ben waited until he was sure that Miss Haining's attention was entirely fixed on the hall below, then darted out and into the shadow. He crouched down, hidden by the table, and looked out between the balustrades. He held his breath, alert to the silhouette of Miss Haining and ready to run if she came his way.

But she too was watching events below. The half-dozen children who had been kept behind were sitting on the bench beside one of the dining tables. Ben could see Sam beside Big Jim at the end of the bench.

The man in the suit was standing by the other table. His voice carried easily to where Ben was hiding.

'I want you all to look at something. That's all. Nothing difficult.'

The girl – he had called her Gemma – was sitting beside the box, her attention fixed on the children opposite. The man took a large black key from his jacket pocket and unlocked the box.

He spoke quietly – so quietly that Ben couldn't hear what he said. Then he leaned across the table and opened the lid of the box. Keeping his eyes on the watching children, he slowly began to tilt the box so they could see inside.

From where he was, Ben could see nothing. Miss Haining was also leaning out, trying to see into the box, but with no more success than Ben.

In the hall below, the children on the bench leaned forward too. Charlie Kleb stood up for a better view. The box tipped further. Further. Until they could all see inside it.

And Sam screamed. One hand to her mouth, eyes wide in terror. Everyone else turned to look at her as she stared transfixed at the box. And screamed and screamed and screamed, like Ben had never heard her scream before.

3

BEN COULDN'T MOVE OR BREATHE. MISS HAINING hurried past him, thumping down the stairs. Sam was screaming, and Mr Magill and the man in the suit were trying to calm her.

The box was still open on the table, but Ben couldn't see inside it. What *was* inside it? What had Sam seen?

The girl, Gemma, closed the lid of the box. The man pointed at the box and said something that Ben didn't hear. Because Sam was *still* screaming. Miss Haining hurried in through the door below the gallery, appearing beneath Ben. Mr Magill yelled at her to get Nurse.

Mr Magill struggled to hold Sam, to stop her arms thrashing about, to calm her down. Ben backed across the gallery, his foot sending the paint pot clattering away. Then he turned and ran down the stairs. Sam's screams echoed after him.

The gallery door was closed. Ben grabbed the handle, turned and pushed in one movement. But the door didn't move. Bolted. He was trapped, and he could still hear Sam screaming and couldn't get to her.

He hammered on the door and yelled, but he knew no one would hear him over the sound of his sister. So he hurried back up to the gallery.

Nurse was standing over Sam. She only worked some days at the home. Other days she was at other homes or schools. But luckily today . . . She turned away and Ben could see the syringe she put into her bag before turning back to Sam.

The screams were subsiding. Sam seemed calmer, but she was still breathing heavily. Whimpering. Her eyes blinking rapidly as her body fought against the sedative.

Below him, Ben could see Mr Magill and the man in the dark suit talking quietly. He caught just a few words and phrases:

'. . . most extreme I've seen . . . definitely right to call me here . . .'

'She can't be moved, not tonight,' Mr Magill replied.

'Tomorrow, then . . .'

Ben didn't hear any more. But he saw that Miss

Haining was standing close to Mr Magill and the man. Was she listening too?

Ben was more concerned about Sam. She seemed to be groggy, leaning against the nurse, who was beside her on the bench. The nurse was talking quietly to Sam and soothing her.

'Help me get the poor girl to her room,' Nurse called.

Mr Magill went to help. Slowly, everyone else left the hall as well. It took a while for Ben to realise that the man in the suit had gone. So had Gemma. And the box.

He waited until the hall was empty, then climbed carefully over the gallery rail. It wobbled a bit, but he hoped it would take his weight. Heart thumping, he lowered himself until he was hanging by his hands from the gallery floor. How far was the drop now? A metre? More than that – two metres?

His arms were tiring, though, and he didn't have any choice. He let go.

The floor slammed into his feet and Ben fell. He tried to roll, but he just jarred his wrist and bruised his side. He got painfully to his feet and limped from the hall.

***

'Ah, Ben. I was just coming to find you.'

Ben bumped into Mr Magill as he was on his way to the girls' block. 'I want to see Sam,' he said. 'How is she? What happened?'

'Calmly,' Mr Magill said, putting a hand on Ben's shoulder. 'She's OK. Had a bit of a turn, as I expect the others told you. But she's going to be all right now. Nurse Muir has given her something to help her sleep.'

'I want to see her,' Ben repeated.

'Maybe later. What she needs now is rest. She'll be fine by the morning. She won't wake until then, and Nurse will keep an eye on her.'

'What happened? Who was that man? What did he do?'

'Oh, it was nothing to do with that,' Mr Magill said quickly. 'How could it be? No one else was taken ill. Just one of those things.' He was leading Ben back to the main house as he spoke. 'She'll be fine soon. Really. The doctor is going to call and check on her. You can see her tomorrow, all right?'

Ben didn't answer. It wasn't all right. But he wasn't allowed in the girls' block and there'd be people still fussing round Sam or checking on her. He'd go over later.

For now he went back to the junior boys' social

room, where he found Charlie Kleb and Big Jim sitting pale-faced.

'How's Sam?' Big Jim asked Ben as soon as he came in.

'Mr Magill says she's fine. Sleeping.'

'Talk about fits,' Charlie said. 'What got into her, do you think? You should have heard her scream.'

'It was the box,' Big Jim said quietly. 'When the man opened the box and tilted it so we could see inside.'

Ben swallowed, his mouth suddenly dry. 'The box,' he said, his voice barely more than a hoarse whisper. 'You have to tell me – what did she see? What was in the box?'

Big Jim and Charlie looked at each other.

'That's just it,' Charlie said. 'There wasn't anything. Nothing at all.'

Big Jim nodded. 'That's right. The box was completely empty.'

After the evening snack – which he didn't really feel like eating – Ben went to ask if he could see Sam. If Mr Magill was in the staff room, maybe he'd relent and let Ben see his sister tonight – even if she was still asleep.

Ben wasn't sure if Sam's sudden 'illness' had anything to do with the man in the suit and his strange wooden box. What had Sam seen inside the empty box? He wondered if the doctor had been yet, and if so what he had said. Mr Magill would tell him.

Except that the staff-room door was closed and no one answered when he knocked. It was late – the day staff must have gone home. The residential staff would be supervising the children. Or at the pub in the village. Or maybe looking after Sam. The girls' block might be out of bounds, but no one could blame Ben for wanting to see his sister when she was ill, could they?

There was a walkway connecting the old house to the new block. Ben ran through it as quickly as he could, because it was open and exposed. The sides were made of glass, so it was also cold in the winter and hot in the summer. But he'd sneaked into Sam's room enough times before to know all the possible hiding places along the way. He might be sure they'd let him see Sam, but he didn't want to ask or explain unless he had to.

The other end of the walkway opened into a foyer with doors leading to the downstairs rooms and a staircase up to the bedrooms. Sam's room was on the second floor.

Ben had only set foot on the first step when he heard someone coming down. Their heels clacked loudly and rhythmically on the concrete steps. A grown-up, by the sound of it. The stairs were fixed on the wall side only. The other side was open, so Ben hurried to hide in the stairwell. He pressed into the shadows, sure that whoever it was wouldn't see him unless they came looking.

He could see the shadow cast across the foyer as the person came down – elongated, thin and gangly. Unmistakably Miss Haining. Ben knew even before he heard her voice.

There was no one with her, so he guessed she was on her mobile.

'He was here, tonight, just like you said . . . With the box you described.' She paused, evidently listening. Then: 'Yes, yes, he did the test . . . Only one, a girl . . .'

She must mean Sam. Who was she talking to? Not the man in the suit who'd brought the box, obviously. Someone else, someone who knew about the box but who hadn't been at the assembly. Ben leaned out, straining to hear but desperate not to be seen. Miss Haining was standing at the bottom of the stairs as she spoke.

'That's right. The girl I told you about, the one in the drawing you showed me . . . He's coming back tomorrow morning, so you'll have to be quick if you want her . . .'

Ben almost gasped out loud. What was going on?

'A thousand – like we agreed.'

Miss Haining ended the call and pushed through one of the doors from the foyer. The door banged shut behind her and Ben could hear her heels clicking on the floor beyond.

He stood for a moment, thinking. But the more he thought, the less sense anything made. The test. The empty box. Some picture of Sam? The only thing he did understand was that Miss Haining had arranged for someone to come and see Sam. He didn't like the sound of it. If anyone was going to be seeing Sam – whoever Miss Haining was speaking to, or the man in the suit – then Ben was going to be there to help her. He'd stay with her all night if necessary, to keep her safe.

Decision made, he ran back through the walkway and all the way through the old house until he reached his own dormitory.

It was almost time for lights-out. Ben stuffed handfuls of clothes and his spare pillow down his bed, pulling the covers up. Then he turned out the bedside lamp and drew his curtain across.

'Cover for me,' he hissed at Jaz in the next cubicle.

'Where you going?' Jaz asked, looking up from his graphic novel.

'I'm going to see if Sam's OK.'

'I heard about that. She threw a real wobbly. Say "hi" from me.'

'Will do,' Ben agreed. 'If anyone comes looking, tell them I've gone to sleep. Say I was tired and upset and it's best to leave me alone. Right?'

Jaz was back in his graphic novel. 'All right. See you later.'

'Yeah,' Ben muttered. 'See you.'

Sam's room was in darkness. Ben didn't want to leave the door open to be able to see, so he turned on the bedside lamp. If a grown-up came in, they would assume another member of staff had done it – or perhaps that Sam had woken for a minute and turned it on herself.

Sam looked calm and peaceful, sleeping easily. Her breathing was regular and Ben just stood listening to her for a while. He reached out tentatively and gently stroked her face. She felt warm and soft and safe.

'Love you, Sam,' he whispered, half expecting her to open her eyes and laugh. But she didn't. The rhythm of her breathing continued uninterrupted.

There was another bed in the room, though Sam didn't share with anyone. The bed wasn't made, but a grey cover was pulled up over the bare mattress. Ben sat down on the spare bed. He couldn't just sit here all night, though. At some point someone would come and check on Sam. He needed somewhere to hide. But just for now . . .

'Can you hear me?' he asked quietly. 'I know you're asleep, but are you *really* asleep?' No reaction. 'You'll stay with me, won't you, Sam? Like we promised, remember? Like we promised by the lake?'

The bedside light flickered slightly and Ben thought he heard something. A clicking, rustling breath of sound. Like someone quietly chuckling.

But there was no one there.

Ben sat watching his sister for a few more minutes, deciding what to do.

'I won't leave you,' he told her.

The covers were crooked and Ben straightened them, pulling the duvet up round Sam's neck so she'd keep warm. There was a dip in the duvet down by her side – like someone had put something heavy down on it. Ben pulled the duvet again. But the dip didn't go away. He smoothed it with his hand.

But as soon as he moved away, the dip was there again. Must be the shape of the bed, he decided.

'Goodnight,' he whispered.

He leaned over and kissed Sam on the cheek. She stirred slightly, but at once her breathing settled back into its pattern. Ben left the light on and slipped underneath the spare bed. He could see the shape of Sam's body beneath the duvet from here. He would stay awake all night, watching her, in case whoever Miss Haining had been talking to came.

But what Ben could not see was the indentation in the duvet down beside Sam. He couldn't see the way the shape changed slightly, as if whatever was making it had moved – had turned to watch Ben and then to check his sister was still sleeping peacefully. If the faint chuckling sound came again, Ben didn't hear it.

And, despite his determination to keep watch all night, within an hour he was fast asleep.

***

The first light of morning was edging round the thin curtains. Ben was instantly awake. He sat up, bumping his head on the bottom of the bed, and stifled a cry. He looked across at Sam's bed, realising he'd been asleep all night, dreading what he might see.

But the shape of the body under the duvet seemed unchanged. Relieved, Ben pulled himself out from under the spare bed and got up. He was cold and stiff from sleeping on the floor and his mouth was dry.

Then he noticed that the bedside lamp had been turned off.

And the shape of the duvet was just that – the duvet. Pulled aside and away from the empty bed.

Sam had gone.

4

THE WHOLE DAY WAS A FOGGY BLUR TO BEN. He remembered it in snatches of movement, moments of action, interludes of silence.

Running from Sam's room, shouting for help. Mr Magill trying to calm Ben down – assuming that Ben had gone early to Sam's room to see how she was. Everyone being sure Sam was not far away. She'd gone to the bathroom, or for early breakfast, or maybe a walk . . . Perhaps she was looking for Ben . . .

Of course no one had taken her away. Why would they? How could they? Ben wanted to tell Mr Magill about Miss Haining, but who could he trust? Mr Magill had brought the man with the box here.

Gradually the growing concern around the home became anxiety, which itself became worry. It was Saturday, so there were no lessons and everyone joined in searching the house and the new block in case Sam had wandered off, still half-sedated and confused, and fallen asleep somewhere.

Then the police arrived.

There were two policemen, asking questions – first of the staff, then later of Ben and the other children. They wanted to know all about Sam and all about the home. Was the main door kept locked at night? Where was the key? Could Sam have opened it? There was no sign of anyone forcing their way in.

The policeman who spoke to Ben was friendly and seemed concerned. He wanted to know how Sam had been – whether she'd been upset about anything, whether she'd mentioned to Ben that she was planning to run away. Ben told him about Miss Haining's phone call, but the policeman didn't seem to think that was important.

'I'll ask her about it, of course. But I expect there's some other quite innocent explanation. Perhaps you misheard.'

'What about the special assembly in the hall?' Ben demanded. 'Did I imagine that too?'

The policeman looked uncomfortable. 'Mr Magill has explained about the assembly and I really can't see it's relevant.'

'It's why Sam had to be sedated. Why she was

asleep and helpless when they came.' Ben didn't tell the policeman that he'd been there – that he'd been asleep. That he should have helped his sister but he'd been asleep and hadn't even heard her being taken.

More police arrived, some with dogs, and started to search the grounds. But Ben knew they wouldn't find Sam. They said they'd circulate her picture. But by lunchtime Ben could tell they were not going to do much more than that.

He overheard the policeman he'd spoken to talking to one of the others.

'Probably another runaway. Teenagers.'

'Wish mine would run away,' the second policeman joked. 'Mind you, if they were shut up in this place, they probably would.'

'Wouldn't we all.'

So that was it, Ben thought. They'd decided Sam had just run off. Like she'd abandon him. She wouldn't. Not ever. They'd promised to stay together.

The man who had brought the box came back in the afternoon. Sitting in the social room, looking out of the window, watching for any sign of Sam, Ben recognised the man's car. It was bright red with a long bonnet, short boot with spare wheel attached, and small doors with old-fashioned handles. The car looked old, but Ben decided it probably wasn't. The top was down, despite the cold.

There was no sign of the girl, Gemma. Just the man, wearing a light-coloured coat over his suit. His dark hair was ruffled by the wind as he drove rapidly up the driveway and skidded to a halt beside the last remaining police car. He was out of the car in an instant, running for the main entrance.

Ben had no trouble finding them. He could hear the man's angry, raised voice as he came down the stairs. Mr Magill's replies were quieter, but still audible. They were in one of the rooms off the corridor that led down to the kitchens.

The door was standing ajar and Ben crept as close as he dared, ready to run if anyone came. Or if the door opened properly.

'Don't you have any security here at all?' the man in the suit was demanding.

'It's a home and school for children no one wants, not a prison,' Mr Magill retorted. 'In any case, that would keep people in, not out.'

'You didn't keep Samantha Foundling in.'

'She was sedated. She didn't leave on her own. *They* knew she was here and they came for her.'

'So how did they know?' the man in the suit wondered.

His voice was quieter, more thoughtful. He seemed concerned about Sam, more than the police had been. He and Mr Magill seemed to know, or at least suspect, who'd taken her.

'Her brother maybe? He's called Ben,' Mr Magill said.

Ben felt cold at the mention of his name. He leaned closer still, his ear almost to the opening between door and frame.

'I don't see how he can be involved. Was he at the test?'

'You sent him out.'

'There you are, then. He doesn't have the Sight.'

'But he might know about his sister's ability. Might have told someone,' Mr Magill said.

'Maybe. But why last night? That's too much of a coincidence. Who else knew how she reacted?'

'The children. Some of the staff who were here. Nurse Muir. But none of them know who you really are. None of them know about the Judgement Box. Only me.'

'Only you . . .' the man echoed.

There was silence for a moment. Then Mr Magill said, 'You surely can't think that I –'

The other man cut him off. 'No, no, no. I trust you, Peter. Really I do.' He sighed. 'Maybe it *is* just a coincidence. Or maybe she really has run away. But I don't think so. I really don't think so.'

Ben could hear them walking towards the door. He looked round for somewhere to hide. The nearest place was the next door along, which was also standing slightly open. He ran to it and ducked inside, looking back into the corridor through the narrowest of cracks.

He watched the man stride off down the corridor towards the main entrance. Mr Magill hurried after him.

'You'll let me know anything that happens,' the man was saying. 'Anything at all.'

'Of course . . .'

Then they were gone. Ben breathed a long sigh of relief. Which became a startled gasp as a voice behind him said, 'And just what do you think you're doing in here, boy?'

He spun round – to find Miss Haining standing there. The room was unused, due to be decorated. Dustsheets covered an old sofa and a low table.

Miss Haining walked slowly towards Ben. 'You were listening, weren't you?'

Ben's mouth dropped open in realisation. 'So were you,' he blurted out. 'You could hear through the wall. You were listening to them.'

'That's quite enough, boy. You're in a lot of trouble, you know.'

Ben shook his head. 'It's you that's in trouble. Who was that man with Mr Magill? And what's happened to my sister?'

'Your sister has run off. Quite possibly to get away from rude boys like you.'

Ben stood his ground as she walked up to him. 'No. Someone took her. And you know who it was.'

Miss Haining blinked. 'Me? What makes you think I know anything about it?' There was a slight hesitation in her voice now. A slight tremble in the hollow skin of her cheek.

'You phoned someone. On your mobile. Last night. Not the man who came today, because he doesn't know where Sam is either. But whoever you spoke to offered you money. Money for Sam.' Suddenly, Ben's wrists were held tight in Miss Haining's brittle hands and he realised he'd been thumping at her. His eyes were watering so much he could hardly see. He tore himself free and ran from the room.

He was halfway down the corridor, sobbing and shaking, when he realised that Miss Haining wasn't following him. She wasn't shouting for him to stop or telling him that he was in big trouble. She hadn't even come out of the room.

Ben wiped his eyes and nose on his sleeve. He breathed deeply, slowly, calmly. Then he tiptoed back to the room.

He didn't dare look inside. He stopped before he got to the door. But he was close enough – he could hear her. She must be on her phone again.

'I know you did, but I didn't have any choice. I had to call.' She sounded impatient and nervous and angry all at once. 'I can't stay here. People are asking questions. I think the girl's brother knows what's going on. And *he* was here again . . . Yes, just now. Talking to Magill.'

She paused, listening. Then suddenly she snapped, 'I don't care about that. I have to leave and to do that I need money. At least the same again. Otherwise I shall have to stay here and before long someone will find out everything . . . I am not threatening you,' she went on, quieter now. 'I'm just warning you. If they get me, they'll get you too. Five thousand – to disappear. But I need it within twenty-four hours.'

Ben had heard enough. He ran back to the entrance hall – and collided with a figure coming the other way.

'Ben! Are you all right?'

'Mr Magill, sir. Yes, I'm fine.'

He hesitated, wondering if he should tell Mr Magill about Miss Haining. But the police hadn't believed him, so why should anyone else? And Mr Magill had brought the man with the box here. He knew more than he was telling Ben.

'We'll find her, really we will,' Mr Magill said.

Ben pushed past Mr Magill. 'I don't think so, sir.'

'Wait! Where do you think Samantha is? Any ideas?'

'She hasn't run off,' Ben told him. 'She wouldn't leave me behind. She wouldn't.'

'We'll find her,' Mr Magill repeated.

Ben could see in the man's eyes that he was sure Ben would never see his sister again. But Ben knew that Mr Magill was wrong. So wrong. He *would* see Sam again – just as she had promised. If not before, he would see her in two weeks – on his birthday, by the lake. He knew, as certainly as he knew anything, that Sam would be there to meet him.

5

THE OTHER BOYS SEEMED TO SENSE THAT Ben didn't want to talk. They said little, but Ben was aware of their sympathy and friendship. He'd never felt so at home here before. Jaz put his hand on Ben's shoulder as he walked past in the social room. He said nothing – didn't need to. Charlie smiled sadly across the room at Ben. Others murmured how sorry they were.

Several of the boys looked in on Ben before lights-out. He was just lying in bed, his mind almost blank.

'You all right?' Big Jim asked, putting his head round the cubicle curtain.

Ben nodded.

'If you need anything, just say.'

'Thanks.'

He thought he'd never get to sleep. But exhaustion crept over him as the rest of the dormitory was still whispering and giggling, fidgeting and settling. He drifted off into a deep, warm sleep. A sleep where Sam was still there, where the man in the suit had never brought his box, where Miss Haining didn't sell children to mysterious people on the telephone . . .

He woke suddenly, still feeling exhausted and tired. It was dark outside his window and the only noise in the dormitory was the collective breathing of the other boys as they slept. Ben sat up in bed. He realised that Miss Haining was the key. She knew who had taken Sam and where she was. He had to confront her and find out what was going on. No one else was going to believe him – not the police, not Mr Magill, no one.

First thing, Ben decided – even before breakfast – he would go over to her room and demand to know what had happened to Sam. Just the thought of talking to her made him feel sick and shaky. But he'd do it – he had to. For Sam.

The window in Ben's cubicle, above his little sink, looked out over the back field towards the woods behind the home. He kept the window slightly open, except when it was really cold. He had come to know all the sounds that crept in during the night. The distant roar of a train if the wind was in the right direction; the hum of traffic on the main road; owls and bats in the wood; the clatter from the kitchens as the staff came on duty and started to get breakfast ready.

But the kitchen staff wouldn't be arriving until after seven. Ben's watch told him it was just gone six in the morning. And the sound he heard was not from the kitchens.

He knew at once what it was. Footsteps – cautious and measured – outside the window. The crunch of gravel on the narrow path at the back of the home. A noise that might have been a high-pitched giggle.

Ben climbed from his bed and looked out of the window. At first he could see nothing except the dark grey of the early morning. Then, gradually, he made out the shapes in the night – the distant trees of the wood, the expanse of grass, the square outline of the new block . . . And a man.

He was walking slowly along the edge of the grass. Ben guessed he'd stepped on to the gravel path by mistake, not seeing it in the dark. Now he was moving silently again, heading for the back door into the new block.

Ben couldn't make out many details. But the man was tall and thin with fair hair and he was wearing a long, loose coat. He looked lopsided, his left shoulder sagging as if under a weight, so that he walked in a slightly ungainly manner. Ben watched him most of the way to the new block. It wasn't the man in the suit – he had been much broader, with black hair. So who was he? And what was he up to?

Without really thinking what he was doing, Ben pulled on his slippers and hurried as quietly as he could from the dormitory. He couldn't be sure that this lopsided man had anything to do with what had happened to Sam, but it would be a coincidence if there wasn't some connection.

He retrieved his coat from the cupboard under the stairs, slipping it over his pyjamas. Then he ran for the connecting walkway that led to the new block.

As Ben neared the end of the walkway he tiptoed, listening for any sound of the intruder. He thought he heard the strange giggling noise again. Possibly the thump of footsteps somewhere further inside the building. But that could be anyone. Holding his breath, he made his way towards the back door – where the man must have come in, if he'd entered the building.

The sound of footsteps grew louder – slow, measured steps along the corridor leading to the staff quarters.

Ben pressed into the shadows at the bottom of the stairs. The man passed close to him, a distinctive silhouette with his shoulder slightly stooped. Ben held his breath, straining to hear as the man murmured something to himself.

'You can find her,' the man said quietly. 'Off you go, my little friend.'

Ben looked round, but there was no one else – just the man. As he watched, the man seemed to straighten up, raising his shoulder as if a weight had been lifted from it. He stood looking up the stairs for a while. Then he turned and walked slowly away, back down the corridor towards the door he had come through.

For a few moments, Ben hesitated. Should he follow the man? Why had he come here, if only to leave again? And who had he been talking to? Was there someone else with him – someone who was already upstairs? Or was he speaking into a microphone for a mobile phone or something?

Slowly and as quietly as possible, Ben started up the stairs. He had never been in this part of the new block before. He knew that some of the live-in staff had their apartments up here. He was tense and scared, ready to turn and run if he heard anyone coming. He could get into so much trouble . . .

Somewhere above him, Ben heard what sounded like a door slam or something fall to the floor. He paused, then carefully continued upwards, reaching a landing. There was carpet on the floor here, with several doors leading off.

Far enough, Ben decided. There was nothing going on. No one was here.

Then the screaming started.

It was like when Sam had screamed. The noise rooted Ben to the spot – a woman's voice, devoid of words and meaning. Containing just fear and pain. Something thumped into one of the doors in front of Ben. He saw the wood rattle in the frame. He shuddered like the door, backing away down the stairs – desperate to turn and run, yet unable to stop looking.

The door was pushed open. It was dark in the apartment behind. A figure staggered out on to the landing – into the light. Miss Haining.

Her greying hair was plastered across her face. Her hands clutched and beat at the air in front of her, as if she was trying to fight off some animal. And she was screaming.

For a moment her eyes latched on to Ben, but he had the feeling she couldn't see him. Her stare was empty and unfocused. Her face was twisted in an agonised frenzy. As Ben watched, transfixed, a line of red appeared down Miss Haining's cheek. As if she'd been scratched. She yelled and spun round, then back again. Her hands were clawing at her own face now as more scratches appeared.

Lights snapped on. The door next to Miss Haining's started to open. There were running feet somewhere on the floor above.

Ben was sure he felt a slight draught – like something pushing past him on the stairway. Between the screaming and the running feet, he could swear he heard someone giggling.

Then he turned and ran down the stairs. He heard the back door of the new block slam shut as he reached the bottom. He raced as fast as he could to his dormitory and dived into bed.

He didn't care that he was still wearing his coat and his slippers. He didn't join the other boys hurrying down to see what was happening when they heard the siren and the ambulance arrived.

He didn't watch as Miss Haining was carried out on a stretcher . . . Her face scratched and torn, her eyes staring and wild, a dribble of saliva running from the corner of her slack mouth.

Ben didn't know that for the rest of her life she would never speak another coherent word. When he did crawl from under his covers and look out of his window, he was sure he could see a man standing in the distance, on the edge of the woods behind the home. A tall, thin, fair-haired man who walked with one shoulder sagging as if it carried a heavy weight.

6

THE DAY AFTER MISS HAINING WAS TAKEN away in the ambulance, Ben went to see Mr Magill.

There was no one else in the maths room and Mr Magill was doing his marking. He glanced up from his desk to see who it was, then smiled sadly and gestured for Ben to come in.

'Leaves a big hole, doesn't it?'

Ben didn't have to ask what he meant. The words summed up perfectly how Ben felt, and the way that Mr Magill said them – his expression, his tone – made Ben wonder who Mr Magill had lost.

'Who was he?' Ben asked.

'Sorry?'

'The man in the suit. The man who came that night with the girl and the box. He had a car that looked old but I don't think it was.'

'Morgan,' Mr Magill said.

'Mr Morgan?'

'No, the car is a Morgan. Hand-built. Lovely. You're right, it's not that old.'

'But the man . . .' Ben insisted. 'You knew him. You brought him here.'

Mr Magill nodded. 'And that's how I know he had nothing to do with Samantha's disappearance. Nothing at all. He wanted to help her, you know. That's why he came here.'

'Can't he help her now? Can't you at least tell me who he was and let *me* ask him if he knows what's happened to Sam?'

Mr Magill stood up. He walked across to Ben and put his hands on the boy's shoulders. 'He can't help. I'm so sorry. Really I am.' Mr Magill looked away, not wanting to meet Ben's accusing stare. 'I'm leaving soon,' he said quietly. 'I've got another job, a long way away.'

'Isn't that a bit sudden? Is it because of the man with the box? Is it because of what happened to Sam?'

Mr Magill shook his head. 'No, not at all. A job came up that I was interested in, that's all.' He went back to his desk and looked down at the exercise book he was marking. 'I'm sorry I can't help you, Ben. But the hole that's been left – it will get smaller.'

He glanced up and just briefly his eyes met Ben's. They both knew he was lying about that as well.

Every day, Sam was there in Ben's mind. He thought about her when he got up in the morning and while he ate his breakfast. He wondered what she was doing as he sat through lessons, and where she was when he stood out in the grounds of the home and stared unseeing into the distance.

He spoke to her, though he knew she couldn't hear. He imagined how she would reply – what she'd say, how she'd look as she said it. Some days he imagined she had her hair tied back. On others it flopped forward, round her face, and she tucked it behind her ear.

But every day, Ben missed her. Every day, his heart felt like it had a heavy, cold stone in it. Every day, the excitement grew as he moved closer to seeing his sister again. On his birthday. By the lake. Like she'd promised.

Two weeks after Sam disappeared, the morning of Ben's fourteenth birthday was cloudy and grey. But to him it felt as if the sun was shining. He could barely wait until the afternoon. He hadn't been back to the lake since Sam went – he didn't want to be there without her. That would be too sad and empty for words.

He could hardly eat any lunch. As soon as the afternoon lessons were over, he slipped away.

'Where are you going?' Jaz asked, seeing Ben get his coat from under the stairs.

'Out.'

'Out where?'

Ben shrugged. 'Just out. That's all.'

'But it's cold. I think it's raining.'

Ben didn't reply. He pulled his coat on and headed for the main door.

'Can I come?' Jaz asked.

Ben shook his head. 'I'd rather be on my own.'

'But it's your birthday. Are you sure you don't want company?'

'Sure.'

Jaz nodded. 'Take care,' he said. 'Don't get daft. See you later, OK?'

'OK,' Ben agreed, and stepped out into the rain.

Ben could feel the anticipation growing within him. He had reached the narrow, muddy path round the lake. In the distance he could see the boarded-up house that he couldn't remember ever living in. He walked faster and faster, breaking into a run as he turned the corner and saw the distant silhouette of the rotting wooden jetty.

And through the rain he saw a figure waiting at the end of the jetty, looking out across the lake. Waiting for him.

'Sam!' he yelled. 'I'm here – I'm coming!'

Ben sprinted full pelt down the slight slope towards the shore. He skidded to a halt, almost slipping over in the mud, as he reached the wooden planking. He could remember Sam's warning a year ago, could hear her voice in his memory as she told him not to go out on the jetty. Then he saw that the figure standing, waiting, was just the broken wooden mooring post sticking up from the broken planks.

Desperate now, Ben looked all round, knowing she was here somewhere, expecting her at any minute to step out of the evening's gathering darkness and grab him in a hug.

But there was no one. Sam wasn't there.

Time seemed to stand still. Only the steady beat of the rain on the wood and the water measured the seconds, the minutes – the hours – that Ben sat there on the side of the jetty.

Finally, as the night closed in around him and the rain slowed again to a persistent drizzle, he wiped the water from his eyes and stood up.

'Hello, Ben,' Sam said.

And his eyes were immediately full of water again. So many tears he could barely see her, so much relief and love he could barely feel her holding him.

'I knew you'd come,' he managed to say between his sobs.

'I said I would. I'll always be here for you Ben. I promised. I'll always be here when you need me. Really I will. I won't be far away.'

'You're not leaving me again?' Ben said, blinking back the tears.

'I have to. I'm sorry. So sorry.'

Ben felt his hand slip from Sam's grasp – like she wasn't really there at all. 'Don't go! I only just found you,' he gasped.

'As often as I can, I'll be here with you.'

She was walking slowly backwards, into the shadows at the edge of the lake.

'Wait! Where are you going? Where will you be? Where *have* you been? When will I see you again?'

Ben ran to catch her. But Sam was shaking her head, biting back the tears. Swallowed up by the darkness under the willow trees by the path.

'I'm sorry, Ben. But I'm glad – so glad I saw you on our special day. Our promise day. And I promise. I *promise* I'll always be here for you, whatever happens. Remember that. *Believe* that.'

Ben stood in the rain, straining to see his sister's pale face in the growing darkness, barely able to make out her silhouette. The movement of her hair as she turned and ran away down the path.

'Happy birthday, Ben. I'll see you soon.'

He thought he could hear her crying. Maybe that was why she had to leave. She always turned away or hid when she wanted to cry. She never let him see the tears or hear the sobs.

'Wait!' Ben yelled. He was running after her, through the shadows, under the drip-drip of the rain off the willow branches. 'Wait, Sam! I promise too. Always – we'll be together always, whatever happens.'

The path was sludge under his feet. The tears were rain in his eyes. And Ben was a shadow in the darkness, running alone.

7

THE ONLY WAY BEN COULD DISCOVER WHAT had happened to Sam was to find whoever had taken her that night. Miss Haining had known, but now she knew nothing at all. The man in the suit who'd brought the box might know, though. Miss Haining had been spying on him and Mr Magill – perhaps to find out how much they did know. He should have told Mr Magill, but the chance had gone now – as had Mr Magill. He'd left for his new job just before Ben's birthday.

Ben couldn't think of any way to track down the fair-haired, lopsided man he'd seen on the night Miss Haining was attacked. So the man in the suit was his only lead. And his only way of finding him was to go to Mr Magill. Sam was out there somewhere. He didn't understand why she'd run away from him, why she'd left him on his own by the lake. But he'd find out.

Discovering where Mr Magill had gone was easier than he expected. He just asked. And Mrs Alten, who was covering the maths teaching, told him.

'Oh, I think he went to a boarding school near Bristol somewhere. Did you want to write to him? How thoughtful. If you give the letter to me I'll pass it on to the office and I'm sure they'll send it for you.'

She probably didn't know the address, or even the name of the school, Ben thought. He considered writing to ask Mr Magill to come and visit him. If he said he knew where Sam was, would that bring Mr Magill and the man with the suit? He thought about it for a long time, then he wrote a short note saying how much he missed Mr Magill and hoped he was enjoying his new job and that Mrs Alten was very nice but didn't give out lollipops.

Ben sealed the note in an envelope he got from Big Jim. The envelope was a distinctive pale blue, but to be sure Ben wrote Mr Magill's name is spiky capitals on the front.

Mrs Alten was as good as her word. The post going out from the home was left in a special tray on the desk in the main office. Ben thought of several different excuses to go to the office during the day. But he needed only one. The corner of a small blue envelope poked out from under a pile of official-looking large brown ones in the tray.

'I think it's Charlie's birthday this week,' Ben told Mrs Trundall. 'I'd like to give him a card, but I want to be sure I get the right day.'

'Why don't you just ask him when it is? Or one of the other boys?'

'I want it to be a surprise.'

Mrs Trundall smiled. 'That's very sweet, Ben. Wait a moment and I'll check for you.'

As soon as she turned away to open the filing cabinet, Ben lifted the brown envelopes. Sure enough, the blue envelope had Mr Magill's name on in Ben's writing and underneath that was the address of the school where he was now working.

'You're right. Charlie's birthday is on Thursday.' Mrs Trundall sat down at her desk again. 'I must remember to wish him a happy birthday myself.'

They received a little pocket money in the home. Not much, but Ben had been saving his for a while. He never spent a lot anyway. Some of the boys had Nintendos and PSPs and spent their money on games for them. But Ben wasn't really into that. He just bought a few books, the odd bar of chocolate or bag of sweets. So even before he started saving, he had some funds.

More than enough for a train ticket to Bristol.

He got the train times off the Internet from the library computer. He decided to catch the last train of the day. That way he shouldn't be missed until morning. Seeing how little effort had been put into hunting for Sam, he didn't think anyone would spend much time trying to track him down. Mrs Alten might recall he had written to Mr Magill, but that was a chance he'd have to take.

Ben drifted off to sleep soon after the train pulled out. He was jolted awake as it left Cheltenham and again a few minutes later at Gloucester. He hadn't really planned much further ahead than getting on the train. He knew there were two stations at Bristol and he wanted the one in the city centre – Temple Meads. But there was no point in trying to find St Humbert's School at gone midnight. He just needed somewhere to wait in the warm until morning . . .

There were several waiting rooms at the station. Ben chose the smallest, where there were only a few other people. A young man was stretched out on one of the bench seats, his head resting on an enormous rucksack. An old woman with a supermarket carrier bag burped and smelt of drink. A man in an expensive coat complained into his mobile that he'd missed the last train and would have to wait until five a.m. for the next one and what was the country coming to and how awful it was and did they call this a *service* when you couldn't even get coffee after midnight, never mind a brandy?

Ben huddled into a fixed plastic seat in the corner of the room and eventually fell asleep.

When he woke, the station was coming to life. His watch told him it was just after half past five. The man with the mobile had gone and a few more people had arrived. A young couple with huge suitcases plastered with tags and airline labels were laughing together.

Ben forced himself to wait a bit longer, then found a taxi at the front of the station. He told the driver the name of the school and the address.

'You'll be a bit early,' the driver joked.

'Extra maths with Mr Magill,' Ben said.

'At seven in the morning? That's keen.'

Ben settled back into the seat as the taxi pulled out into the start of the early-morning rush hour.

'What do I say to Mr Magill?' he wondered.

Ben saw that the driver's eyes were fixed on him in the rear-view mirror. Had he spoken out loud?

'You all right back there?'

'Fine, thanks.'

Ben waited outside the school gates until it was half past eight. Although it was a boarding school, some children obviously came each day. Ben tagged on to the back of a group of children who arrived together and walked up the long drive from the road. The main school building was red brick, imposing and Victorian. It was a bit like the home, only less forbidding and better cared for.

Ben followed the signs for 'Reception' to a large wooden door. Inside was an entrance hall with another door leading into an office. The door was wedged open so the lady at the desk could see anyone who came in.

'Can I help you?' she called. 'Sorry – I don't think I know your name.'

'It's Ben. Ben Foundling.' He went into the office. She looked like a kind lady, with grey hair and glasses hanging on a chain round her neck.

'Foundling.' She frowned. 'Have you just started this term?'

'I need to see Mr Magill. It's very urgent.'

The woman's frown had deepened as she absorbed the details of Ben's appearance. His coat was crumpled from being slept in and he didn't have the same bright blue blazer as the other boys he'd seen arriving.

'I have to see Mr Magill,' Ben repeated. 'He teaches here. He's new.'

The woman barely took her eyes off Ben as she picked up the phone on the desk.

'It's Miss Flecker. Could you see if Mr Magill is still in the staff room and ask him to come to the office. I think it might be rather important. He has a . . . visitor.'

There were two armchairs in a little waiting area in front of the desk, but Ben didn't sit down. He stood and waited while Miss Flecker got on with her work, glancing up at him occasionally.

Several minutes later, Mr Magill appeared and was more than surprised. 'Ben! What on earth are you doing here?'

'I needed to see you, sir.'

'You *do* know this boy?' Miss Flecker asked.

Mr Magill nodded. 'I, er, used to teach him. Perhaps you could give us a minute, Miss Flecker?'

He waited for Miss Flecker to give a loud sniff and leave, then nudged the wedge out from under the door with his foot and let it swing shut.

'So what's going on, Ben? Does anyone know you're here?'

Ben shook his head.

There was silence for several moments. Then Mr Magill sighed. 'Are you in trouble? Some problem at the home?'

Ben shook his head again, not trusting himself to speak.

Mr Magill sighed again. He took a mobile phone out of his pocket and flipped it open, holding it up and staring for several seconds at it. Just as the man in the suit had done.

'It's Sam,' Ben blurted out.

'Sam? Have they found her?'

Ben hesitated. Should he tell Mr Magill he'd seen Sam?

'Look,' Mr Magill went on, 'I'm going to ring your housemaster at the home, Mr Logan, and tell him you're here and that you're safe. Then we can arrange to get you back. I can maybe get you something to eat here. OK?'

Ben looked down at his feet. This wasn't going well, but he didn't know what to do or say. It had all seemed so simple when he set off. All he had to do was find Mr Magill and ask him about the man in the suit, or if he knew yet what had happened to Sam. But now he didn't dare say a word.

He felt Mr Magill's reassuring hand on his shoulder. 'You can wait here. Take a seat for a minute, because I need to make a couple of calls.'

Ben slumped down into one of the armchairs, while Mr Magill stepped out into the corridor. Ben could hear him talking on his mobile phone. He couldn't catch the whole conversation – just enough to know he was in trouble and he was going back to the home.

His mind drifted off. Where was Sam? How could he ever find out about the man in the suit now? He had to ask – when Mr Magill came back, he'd ask him about the man in the suit. He'd demand to know who the man was and what he knew about Sam and the people who'd taken her away.

Suddenly, something was different. Maybe it was the tone of Mr Magill's voice. But Ben could tell he was talking to someone else now – not the police or Mr Logan at the home.

'Yes, just turned up here . . .' Mr Magill was

saying. 'No sign of the girl, and the boy's showing no sort of ability . . .' He lowered his voice further and Ben couldn't hear any more.

What should he do now? What would Sam do? What would she say? Ben tried to pretend she was there with him in the room.

'He's talking to the man in the suit,' Ben whispered, imagining he was talking to Sam.

He imagined he could hear her reply. 'You need to get hold of his phone.'

'Why do I need his phone?'

'Ben?'

He leapt to his feet in surprise. 'Mr Magill.'

'I thought I heard you talking to someone.'

There was a chill breeze against Ben's neck and he realised that the office window was open. He could hear the sound of traffic from outside.

'Just thinking out loud, sir. And I was thinking . . .'

'Yes?'

'I was thinking that I've been very stupid,' he lied. 'It was just . . . You know.'

'We all have stupid moments.' Mr Magill smiled. 'Whatever's wrong, Ben, we can get it sorted out. All right?'

Ben nodded. 'All right. I'd like to call Mr Logan at the home. To say sorry.'

'I think that's a very good and sensible idea.'

'Thank you.' Ben held out his hand, hoping that Mr Magill wouldn't just tell him to use the office phone on the desk.

But, perhaps instinctively, Mr Magill handed Ben his mobile. And Ben could see in the man's eyes that he regretted it immediately.

Ben took the phone and turned quickly away, as if embarrassed.

Mr Magill seemed to understand this and said, 'I'll give you a minute. It'll be fine.' Then he patted Ben gently on the shoulder, smiled reassuringly and left the room.

The phone was quite complicated. It had a menu of small icons – many of which Ben didn't understand. But he managed to find the call register and the list of calls made.

The last was simply: 'Knight'.

'Check in the contacts list or address book or whatever it has,' Sam would have suggested. 'See if there's an address.'

There was: *Knight – Gibbet Manor, Hangman's Lane, Dartmoor.*

Ben closed the phone and put it down on the desk. It would be useful to keep it, but that was stealing. And mobile phones could be tracked, couldn't they?

The wedge from the door was lying on the floor. Ben pushed it under the door and kicked it into place, jamming the door shut. Then he climbed out of the open window.

He didn't know how long he had before Mr Magill realised he'd gone. But he did know where he was heading now. For the first time since Sam had disappeared, Ben felt he was in control.

8

OF COURSE, IT WASN'T QUITE THAT SIMPLE. BEN had a name and an address. But he had no idea where Hangman's Lane was and Dartmoor was a big place. He didn't like to think about what would happen if this man, Knight, knew nothing about Sam. But he knew that Knight had been worried about her – so surely he'd help Ben find Sam, even if he knew nothing . . . At last he was doing something. He was making progress. He'd find her again no matter what it took, or how long he had to search.

Ben didn't want to spend his money on another taxi. Even though it was a long walk back into the centre of Bristol, it was still early – the school run had barely ended and the streets were busy with cars taking people to work. By the time he found a shopping centre with a bookshop it was almost eleven o'clock.

The bookshop was one that had a coffee area. Ben bought himself a Coke from a bored, spotty young man who barely glanced at him, then found a good-sized table. He'd already bought a notebook and a pencil, but he didn't want to have to buy the road atlas or detailed Ordnance Survey map he'd found.

His first task was to find Hangman's Lane and this took longer than he had expected. It wasn't in the index of the road atlas and there was no place name in the address – it could be any small stretch of road on Dartmoor. He unfolded the OS map and began to work across it, searching for Hangman's Lane.

Eventually, he found it. A winding, narrow white line that ended at a cluster of dark buildings. Could that be Gibbet Manor? The road atlas was no help – it showed the whole area as empty 'National Park'. But Ben made a rough sketch in his notebook of where the major towns were in relation to Hangman's Lane.

The nearest place was Princetown, which didn't seem to be on a railway. It looked like the nearest train station must be in Plymouth. Would there be a bus from there? A rough measurement told him that it was fifteen miles from Plymouth to Princetown. Then another seven or eight to get to Hangman's Lane.

A lady was clearing away the used coffee cups and plates. She took Ben's empty Coke glass and wiped round his map and notebook.

'Shouldn't you be in school?'

Ben hadn't thought of that. 'Er – we have a day off today,' he said. It sounded lame even to him.

But the woman just nodded. 'More days off than days on. Had my two at home last week. Training day. This some homework?'

'Sort of.'

'At least they give you something to do.' She turned her head sideways to look at the OS map. 'Dartmoor. Where the prison is. *Hound of the Baskervilles* country.'

'Sherlock Holmes?' Ben hadn't read the book, but he knew of the story. 'Are you sure?'

The woman nodded. 'I work in a bookshop. Well, in a coffee shop in a bookshop. But if you go to Dartmoor, you watch out for the hound.' She winked, laughed and bustled off.

The train was expensive and Ben didn't have enough money. He found out the prices from an automated ticket machine at Temple Meads station. Checking the timetables gave him an idea of the route the train took to Plymouth and he played around with the machine until he found he could afford to get as far as Exeter St David's and still have a little emergency cash.

It actually wasn't far from there to Plymouth. Maybe no one would check his ticket. But if they did, he'd pretend he'd fallen asleep and missed his stop.

There was a train at 12.44 and the man in the ticket office told him it would take about an hour to get to Exeter. Ben already knew that from the timetable – just as he knew it would arrive in Plymouth about another hour after that.

But what would he do when he arrived at Plymouth? There would be maybe a couple of hours before it got dark and he had almost no money to get to Princetown . . .

Ironically, Ben really did sleep through Exeter. But no one came to check tickets. At Plymouth he avoided the automatic barriers and followed a woman with a child in a buggy. He helped her get the buggy down from the train to the platform and kept close as they went through a gate opened by a man in uniform.

The woman fumbled for her tickets and Ben handed his across at the same time, making sure it was under the woman's. The man at the gate glanced at the top ticket and waved them through together.

'I don't suppose you know how I can get to Princetown?' Ben asked the woman.

It was a long shot, but maybe that was where she was going and she'd give him a lift. But it wasn't.

'I think there's a bus,' she said. 'You'll have to ask.'

The bus cost Ben the last of his money. If he wanted to return to Plymouth he'd have to find some more money from somewhere. Or walk. He was going to have to walk across the moors from Princetown to Hangman's Lane anyway.

After about ten minutes, the bus turned off the main road on to a narrower, winding lane. He was warm and safe as he sat staring out of the window, but the grey-green moorland was forbidding and windswept. Dark clouds were rolling in across a grey sky.

Princetown seemed grey as well, in the dying light. A pale moon struggled through the edges of dark clouds, barely illuminating the lane that Ben took out of town. It wasn't quite five o'clock yet, but it was black as midnight.

Ben hummed to keep himself company. It was so dark that a couple of times he almost walked off the narrow road and into the ditch beside it. Only the change of texture under his feet saved him from a muddy fall.

He walked for well over an hour before he found the turning to Hangman's Lane. The moon emerged for the briefest of moments to shine across the faded finger-signpost. Ben thought this was the first piece of luck he'd had since he got to Plymouth – he could easily have missed the turning and walked on into the middle of nowhere. How far along Hangman's Lane was Gibbet Manor? He hoped it would be only a hundred metres, but he feared it would be more . . .

Almost as soon as he had turned on to the single-track lane, he felt he was being followed. He stopped and turned round, but there was no one there. Just shadows. Then the first spots of rain started to fall.

Ben walked on. He didn't feel like humming any more. The cold wind was pulling at his coat and eating into his fingers and his ears. Rain splashed on his face. And he was still sure there was someone there. He spun round sharply.

Again, just the shadows. The silhouette of the hedge beside the lane. Ben stared hard at the darkest area, as if he could banish the darkness by concentrating hard enough. Was there something – something moving? The hedge rustling in the wind?

He set off again, but his every footstep seemed to be followed by the faintest echo. As if someone – or some*thing* – was taking care to match him step for step.

Suddenly, the whole lane was lit by an explosive flash. A silent blast of light, so bright it dazzled Ben. He shrieked in surprise and sudden fear – his cries drowned out by the percussive clap of thunder that lagged a few seconds behind the lightning.

He was drenched in seconds. Running from whatever was behind him. Sprinting towards whatever lay ahead.

Another flash – and Ben was sure that there was something keeping pace with him. A glimpse, a hint, a suggestion of a shape scuttling up the lane. The skidding click of claws on the slippery surface . . .

'Who are you?' he yelled into the returning darkness. 'What do you want?'

The sky turned white with another huge flash. Ahead of Ben, standing in the middle of the lane, just at the point where it turned and sloped away down the hill, a figure was standing. He saw her as clear as day for the flickering instants of the lightning.

'Sam!'

He ran full pelt, rain streaming into his eyes. At the point where she'd been standing, he slowed, looking all round. Waiting for the next flash of inevitable lightning.

But when it came, there was no one in sight.

Confused and cold and frightened, Ben walked slowly onwards, down the shallow incline and into the deepening shadows. There was no sign of Sam, and he knew he must have imagined her, must have thought he'd heard her voice.

The rain was no longer as heavy. The lightning was weakening. The moon had managed to break through and there was enough light now for Ben to see the house ahead of him. Black against the dark grey clouds and picked out by the lightning, it was just a shape with no detail or character. A cutout.

Huge iron gates barred the lane thirty metres ahead of Ben. They hung from stone posts set in a high wall. The lane went on past the gates, continuing up an incline so that the house was visible above the curling ironwork. In the centre of each gate was an ornate scaffold – upright, crossbar and noose, like from a child's game of Hangman.

Ben stood for a moment staring up at the gates and the house beyond. It had to be Gibbet Manor.

Before starting up the lane again, he looked round. It was just an instinct. He hadn't heard or seen anything. But one glance behind was enough. Something was hurtling towards him – bounding down the lane. The air was filled with the sound of the creature's growls. For a moment, Ben couldn't move.

'*Hound of the Baskervilles* country,' the woman in the bookshop had said.

Without knowing it, Ben had started to run. He was racing towards the gates, desperate to keep ahead of the hellhound coming after him. But he knew, absolutely *knew*, that the gates would be locked even before he reached them.

The iron was cold and wet under his hands. He could feel rust flaking off as he heaved and pushed. To no effect. A thick metal chain was looped through the gates, binding them together and holding them shut. An enormous padlock hung on the other side, out of Ben's reach.

He turned. The darkness seemed to have gathered itself into a living thing – a black shape that leapt at Ben. Black paws lashed out at him. Oily, rancid breath clawed at his nostrils. He thrust his arms out to protect himself and felt the matted warm pelt of the shadows.

9

THEN SUDDENLY BEN WAS FALLING backwards. Strong arms dragged him through the narrow gap between the gates before slamming them shut again. The chain was pulled tight. Ben lay on his back, staring up at the gates from the other side now.

Just a pair of wrought-iron gates, held shut by a chain and a padlock, dripping from the rain. With nothing and no one to be seen beyond them.

'Are you all right, son?'

Ben struggled quickly to his feet and turned to face whoever had opened the gates and pulled him through. A torch shone full in Ben's face, dazzling him so that all he could see behind it was the vague shape of a man.

'Fine, I think. Thank you. But what was that . . . that thing?'

As the man lowered his torch, Ben could see now that he was short and stocky. His thinning grey hair was plastered across his scalp by the rain.

'The gates are kept locked at night. Don't want anything getting into the estate. Nothing that doesn't have business here, anyhow. Do you have business here?'

'I've come to see Mr Knight.'

The man nodded. 'That isn't what I asked. But whether he sees you or not is up to him.'

He reached out, and it took Ben a moment to realise he meant to shake hands.

'Pendleton Jones,' the man said. There was a trace of accent in his voice, a rural edge to it. 'I look after the grounds. Like I said, things try to get in. The gates and the wall stop most of them. I lay traps for the others.'

He turned and started up the drive towards the house.

'Things?' Ben hurried to catch up. 'What sort of *things*?'

'Things like the one that tried to get you. Some aren't so vicious. Others are much more dangerous.'

'But – what was it?'

'What did you see? What did you think it was?'

Ben wasn't sure. 'Shadows. I don't know. But it felt . . .' He shook his head.

'Anyone could get that much of an impression of it. A manifestation like that, you don't need the Sight to feel its breath on the back of your neck.' The man paused and turned to look at Ben again, shining his torch up and down as if assessing him. 'If that's all you saw, then you're nothing special.'

'Oh, thanks,' Ben muttered. He started walking again.

The man made no move to follow, just standing where he was, watching. 'Best not tell Mr Knight about it or he'll know you're nothing special too. In fact,' he called after Ben, 'best not to mention you've even spoken to me. Keep him guessing about how you got inside the gates. Good luck, son.'

Ben felt no sense of achievement as he approached the large building. Only dread. The house seemed to sprawl across the landscape, as if it had been thrust up out of the earth rather than built. The frontage was weathered and cracked, ivy spreading across it like veins. The pale moonlight cast sinister shadows and exaggerated the pallid stone surrounding the windows.

There was a rusting metal rod hanging down beside the dark wooden door. It ended in a loop of a handle, which Ben pulled. Deep inside the house he heard a bell jangle in reply.

He waited what seemed an age. Light was seeping round the edges of heavy curtains at the windows, so he guessed there was someone in. Eventually he heard the muffled sound of footsteps rapidly approaching the door. This was followed by the rasp of bolts drawing back and the thunk of a heavy lock, then finally the door swung inwards.

The woman was holding a mobile phone. She glanced at the screen before putting it away in her jacket pocket. She was wearing a smart dark trouser suit and looked about the age Ben's mother might have been. Her hair was icy blonde, cut short like a schoolboy's and scraped back from her face and forehead.

'Is it still raining?' she asked. Her voice was gentle and calm.

Ben shook his head. 'I have to see –'

'Mr Knight, yes,' she interrupted. 'You'd better come in. You'll catch your death out there. Look at you.'

'Thank you.' Ben hurried inside, aware he was

dripping on the wooden floor. But the woman seemed not to notice. 'My name . . .' he began.

'. . . is Ben Foundling,' the woman finished for him. 'Of course it is. Come with me and let's get you dry and find you some hot soup. Mr Knight is busy just now, but I'll let him know that you're here.'

Ben followed the woman through a dimly lit hallway. There were wooden panels and dark paintings on the walls – some portraits, some landscapes, one a bizarre picture of a demon sitting on a bed beside a sleeping woman.

The woman's high heels clicked on the floor as she led the way briskly down a corridor. Ben wondered who she was, but just as he was about to ask her, she said, 'I'm so sorry, Ben, I didn't introduce myself. You must think me very rude. I'm Mrs Bailey. I look after the house and manage Mr Knight's business. I look after the other children too.'

'Other children?'

The corridor ended at a large kitchen. One wall was taken up with a wide black cooking range. There was a bare wooden table in the middle of the stone-flagged floor. Saucepans and other cooking utensils hung on racks from the ceiling. A microwave stood incongruously on a worktop, close to an equally out-of-place large aluminium fridge.

'Soup,' Mrs Bailey declared. 'And if you sit here by the range, you'll soon warm through.'

She pulled a chair out from the table and angled it for Ben to sit in.

Ben was shivering. He hadn't realised how cold – and afraid – he was until he felt the warmth from the stove. He almost collapsed into the chair, the sleeve of his jacket catching a china jug close to the edge of the table as he moved.

But Mrs Bailey's hand was already outstretched, ready to catch the jug before it fell. She must have seen what was about to happen. She steadied the jug, moving it out of the way.

'I'll get you some soup first. Then I'll tell Mr Knight you're here,' she said.

The warmth from the range slowly seeped into Ben's bones. His hands were cupped round a mug of thick vegetable soup. It was so hot from the microwave that he could only sip at it. But the soup was tasty and before long Ben was feeling much better.

He wished Sam was with him. When he looked up from his soup and saw there was a figure watching from the door to the corridor, for the briefest moment he thought it *was* Sam.

But it was the girl who had come with Knight to the home. Gemma. She was leaning against the door frame, her arms folded, head tilted to one side. There was someone else behind her, another child Ben couldn't see clearly. He could just make out that it was a boy – dark-skinned, with pale eyes that gleamed in the shadows.

'He doesn't have any aura at all,' Gemma said to the boy, as if Ben wasn't there. 'Why's he come?'

Ben wasn't sure what to say. Didn't she know he could hear what she said.

Another voice – an older girl's – called from back down the corridor. It sounded bossy and irritated. 'Come away from there. You're not supposed to be down here. Come on.'

The boy turned and walked quickly away. Gemma pushed herself away from the door frame with a nudge of her shoulder.

'See you,' she said to Ben, and smiled. Then she turned and ran after the boy.

Moments later, another girl appeared – Ben guessed it was the girl who had called out to them and told them to go away. She was older – older than Sam too. Her dark hair hung in curls to her shoulders and she had the kind of mouth that curled downwards in a sort of perpetual sneer.

'Have you come to look at me as well?' Ben asked.

She sniffed. 'Yes,' she said. 'Though I don't know why I bothered.'

Ben turned away, taking a sip of his soup. When he looked back, she had gone.

The man in the suit arrived a few minutes later.

Knight's study was a mixture of the orderly and the chaotic. There were piles of books and papers, shelves of books and CDs and DVDs and computer disks. Almost every surface seemed to be covered. Display cases contained everything from fossils to a long-bladed knife, gold coins to a human skull, a roll of yellowed parchment tied with faded red ribbon to intricate figures carved from bone or ivory . . .

Ben noticed little of it. He sat nervously on the edge of an upright chair in front of Knight's enormous mahogany desk. The top of the desk was the only surface that was relatively clear – a leather-bound notebook, a closed laptop computer, a mobile phone, a pad of paper and a silver fountain pen.

Behind the desk, Knight leaned back in his chair, his elbows resting on the wooden armrests, his fingertips touching.

'Ben Foundling,' he said thoughtfully. 'If you're looking for your sister, I'm afraid I can't help you.'

'I think you can,' Ben said, surprised at how defiant and confident he sounded.

'Not directly. But there are other ways.' Knight leaned forward, transferring his elbows to the desk as he regarded Ben carefully. 'Gemma tells me you have no aura at all. Certainly I saw nothing when we met the other week. Your sister, though . . .' He frowned. 'Or are you so powerful it's somehow hidden from us? Is that it?'

ds

'Before I tell you anything, I need to know what your abilities are. Your potential. I didn't even test you before, did I?'

Ben remembered watching from the gallery – the test with the box. Knight couldn't know he'd seen what happened. So he said nothing.

Knight tapped his fingertips together several times before seeming to make up his mind. 'Wait here a moment,' he said. 'I won't be long.' He got to his feet and strode from the room, leaving the door slightly open behind him.

'What do I do?' Ben murmured out loud. If he failed this test, Knight would send him back to the home . . .

He wondered what Sam would do. But then he realised he didn't need to wonder. He'd already seen the test. He knew what she'd done.

Ben gasped as he felt a hand on his shoulder. Startled, he turned sharply – and saw it was Gemma. She was looking down at him sadly.

'He'll send you back,' she said quietly. 'Why did you come here?'

Ben said nothing. The girl shrugged and walked over to the desk. A few moments later, Knight returned. He was carrying the wooden box that Ben remembered from the home. He put it down carefully on the desk.

'I'm going to ask you to look at something, Ben,' Knight said. 'That's all. Nothing difficult.'

It sounded like a well-rehearsed speech, something the man had said a hundred times to a thousand children over the years . . .

Ben nodded, not daring to speak. But he forced himself to look at Knight, and Gemma, and the box.

Knight was holding the large key. He unlocked the box and murmured a few words. Ben caught only some of them: '*Effrego expositus libere . . .*'

Then Knight carefully lifted the lid. Ben stood up, so he could see. Knight tilted the box forward slightly so that Ben could see right inside. Gemma was watching Ben intently, like a hunting animal.

Ben thought back to when Sam did the test. He remembered watching from the gallery as Knight opened the box.

The empty box. Just like Charlie and Big Jim had told him, it was *completely* empty.

Ben put his hands to his face, still staring into the box, and screamed for all he was worth.

10

HE SCREAMED SO HARD HIS EYES WATERED. Tears ran down his face and his stomach was heaving. But Ben could see Knight nodding with grim satisfaction. Mrs Bailey was there, running to take Ben's arm and lead him away. Someone – another grown-up – took his other arm, but he didn't see who it was. He just concentrated on the screaming until his throat was raw and his lungs were exhausted.

It wasn't just his lungs that were exhausted. Slipping away from the home the previous night seemed weeks ago. His legs could barely support him now as he was helped upstairs. Ben collapsed on to a soft bed. Mrs Bailey pulled a duvet up over him and he was asleep before she let go.

Hours, or perhaps days, later Ben woke. He was still tired. The curtains were drawn, so he guessed it was dark outside. But the bedside light was on. He was in a large bed in a big square room. The room was sparsely furnished – just a bedside locker, a little dressing table with a mirror, a chest of drawers and a narrow wardrobe. All the furniture was made from a dark, reddish wood.

Gemma was sitting on the edge of Ben's bed, swinging her feet. She spoke without looking at him.

'What do you see?'

'Just a room,' he said, confused. 'What should I see?'

'No. What do you *see*?'

Ben pulled himself up so he was sitting and looked round again.

'You're funny,' Gemma said. Now she did look at Ben, and she smiled. 'I see *everything*,' she said, and there was sadness in her words. 'But you're all right here, at the school. Nothing can get in unless Mr Knight lets it. What you saw inside the box can't get out. It's sealed in tight. Actually, I think it likes it in there. Scaring kids who can see it.'

Ben didn't answer. He didn't want to give her any clue that he hadn't actually seen anything in the box.

'I didn't used to like to talk about it,' Gemma went on. 'None of us did. But you're safe here with us. With your friends.' She jumped down from the bed and gave him a quick wave and a grin. 'Bye.'

He drifted off to sleep again. This time he was woken by the sound of whispering close by.

'His *sister*?' a voice was saying. It had a faint accent.

'That's what Gemma said. Anyway, we shouldn't be here.'

Ben sat up again, rubbing sleep from his eyes. 'Who are you – what do you want?' he demanded.

A boy and a girl were standing there. He'd seen them both before, when he was drinking his soup in the kitchen. The boy looked Indian, with a round face and short black hair that was spiky at the front. He seemed to be a bit older than Ben. The girl was about eighteen, he thought, and still had a half-sneer as she stared back at Ben.

'I'm Rupam,' the boy said. 'This is Maria.'

'What are you doing here? What do you want?'

'We could ask you that,' Maria said. 'Why did you come?'

'I want to know what happened to my sister,' Ben said. They'd mentioned Sam – maybe they knew something.

But the girl just shrugged. 'Never met her.'

'Gemma might know,' the boy – Rupam – suggested.

'She doesn't know anything,' Maria snapped, and Ben sensed that Rupam's comment had annoyed her. 'We shouldn't be here,' she said again, turning and walking briskly from the room.

Rupam grinned at Ben and gave him a wave. 'See you.'

Mrs Bailey brought Ben clean clothes and told him that Mr Knight would like to see him as soon as he felt up to it.

Ben swallowed. He nodded but said nothing. Had he been found out? Did they realise he was here under false pretences – wherever here was and whatever he was pretending?

There was a bathroom next door to Ben's room. He had a shower and changed his clothes. He was feeling more awake now. He wondered where Sam was right now . . .

Knight was waiting for him in a large drawing room at the back of the house. A log fire was burning enthusiastically in a large open grate. Knight sat in an armchair, his legs outstretched, reading a book. As Mrs Bailey led Ben into the room, Knight closed the book and set it down on a small table beside his chair. Ben couldn't read the title – it was printed in faded gold on the scuffed leather binding.

'Well now, young man,' Knight said, gesturing for Ben to sit in the chair on the other side of the stone fireplace. 'Have you come to join us?'

'I've come to find out what happened to Sam.'

'Your sister?'

Ben nodded. 'You tested her, with that box. Then she disappeared.'

'I had nothing to do with that,' Knight said quietly. 'And, although it probably doesn't help, I'm very sorry.'

Ben looked away, staring at the flickering shapes of the flames in the hearth. 'I know. I heard you talking to Mr Magill.'

Knight said nothing for several moments. The silence was broken only by the crackling of the burning wood. Ben glanced at Knight and saw that he too was staring into the flames.

'The Judgement Box,' Knight said at last, 'tells me if the children I test have an ability. If they can *see*. Most can't, of course. But some, a few, have the ability. Maybe they live with it every day. Or maybe they don't even know they have it. You, for example . . .'

He turned to look at Ben. His eyes were deep and dark, and Ben felt the man could see into every corner of his mind.

'Me?'

'You saw what was in the box. But I get the impression it isn't a constant ability. You have . . . something. Some talent, evidently. Potential that can be unlocked.'

'What about Sam?' Ben demanded.

'Ah . . . Your sister was unique. Even I could see she had an aura, an ability. And it's years since . . .' He sighed and turned away again, staring at the fire once more. 'I think your sister had a far stronger ability, a far clearer Sight, than anyone else I have come across. Even Maria when she was younger. Even Gemma.'

'How do you mean?'

'I mean she saw them *all the time*. Every waking moment. It must have affected her very deeply. When did she start?' he asked.

'Start?' Ben wasn't sure what he was talking about.

'When did she start to see the demons? The ghosts? The dead?'

As soon as Knight said it, Ben knew he was right. He knew she saw something, but he hadn't realised exactly what it was. But now he knew that Sam had seen demons and ghosts – each and every day. By the lake, on the bus, in the home . . . She'd even told him once, he realised. He had laughed and she'd never mentioned it again.

'She always saw them. Since forever,' he said. 'What is this place? What do you do here? *Who are you?*'

Knight smiled. 'We do have an official title. But everyone calls us the School of Night. I suppose it's flattering in a way. I set it up . . . so long ago. After I lost my own ability . . .'

He stood up and walked slowly round the back of his chair. He turned so he had his back to the fire.

'When we are young, we see as children.' He smiled. 'I know it sounds obvious. But there is an innocence, a naivety, a willingness to believe that we lose as we grow older. Maybe it's to do with adolescence, or perhaps it's just that we learn what we should and shouldn't believe in. Like ghosts – how many adults believe in ghosts? I mean really *believe* in them? Yet almost every child is open to the idea. That's why it's the children who see them. It's a world that is later closed off by experience and by reason and logic.'

Ben leaned forward in the chair. 'You said this place is a school?'

'We're between intakes now. But usually there

are up to a dozen children here. Sometimes more. The most gifted, the ones with the real Sight. We train them to fulfil their potential – so they can be at the forefront of the battle.'

Ben gaped. 'Battle?'

'Most ghosts and spirits are harmless enough. After-images, souls that got left behind. We can help them find rest . . . But some – some are the creatures of Hell itself. And it's our job to send them back there.'

Ben could hardly believe what he was hearing, but the man seemed deadly serious.

'And that would have been Sam's job?'

'Oh yes. I don't know what happened to Sam, but like you I want to find out. She was going to come here. She would have been one of our most powerful soldiers. Like Gemma, she could see *everything*, all the time. Unfortunately that made her a potential threat to those who don't want us to exorcise the ghosts and banish the demons. And that's why I think they took her.'

'But who took her? And where?' Ben was on his feet. 'We have to help her – if she's in danger!'

Knight put his hand on Ben's shoulder, calming him. 'We shall do what we can. But it's been some time now, Ben. She could be . . . anywhere.'

'I saw her,' Ben blurted out, though he'd meant to keep it secret. 'By the lake, on my birthday. At least . . .' He hesitated. The more he thought about it, the more uncertain he was of what he had seen. Had Sam really been there? Had he wanted her to keep her promise so badly that he'd just imagined it? 'I thought I saw her,' he said. 'By the lake. And again on the way here. Only a glimpse. But . . . Maybe it was just wishful thinking.'

'It happens,' Knight said softly. 'When we are hurt so badly, sometimes our minds pretend the hurting is over and that everything's OK again.'

'Will you send me back to the home?'

'Do you want me to?'

He wasn't sure what he was letting himself in for, but Ben was sure his best chance of finding Sam was to stay close to Knight. Maybe he could persuade the man to organise a proper search. Not like the police.

'No,' he said. 'I don't want to go back there.'

'*This* is your home now, Ben,' Knight said. 'You're very lucky. Most of the children we train don't come here to be taught how to use their abilities and what they can do to help. They are identified by agents we have in the schools and the homes, like where you were.'

'Mr Magill,' Ben realised. 'He was working for you all the time!'

'And he noticed Sam, so he called me. There were several children at the home with potential, but Sam was the most remarkable. Usually, the children who can *see* are encouraged to develop their powers in secret. At after-school clubs and in tutorials when everyone else thinks they're learning how to type or doing extra French or playing chess. We have a network of teachers and mentors who train them up, and the children report what they *see* – the ghosts and the spirits and the demons.'

'And then what?'

'As I said, most of the creatures are harmless. But some must be dealt with – either by the children themselves or, in extreme cases, with help from people trained here at the School of Night. Above all, though, our work is secret from most people, and it must stay that way.'

'Why? Surely if people knew . . .'

'Can you imagine? There would be an outcry, then panic or, worse, denial and we'd be closed down. Not everyone believes in what we do. There are always those who think they can tame the demons, that they can use them to further their own aims, to gain influence and wealth. People who will risk everything – their lives, their souls, the *world* – in the search for power.'

Ben felt as if his head was spinning from trying to absorb so much information. 'And these people took Sam?'

'I'm afraid it's likely.'

'But why? What did they want with her? Did she escape? And where is she now? Have they taken her again?'

Knight sighed. 'I really don't know. And you have so much to learn, Ben. In fact, it's time you started. I'll introduce you to the other children. As I say, we only have a few pupils here at the moment, until the next intake. But you can start at once.' He rubbed his chin as he considered. 'Yes, I think you can start this afternoon. Gemma and I have a job to do, with the help of a good friend of ours. He could manage it on his own, of course, but I need to see him anyway. You can come too and see what we get up to.' Knight's eyes widened slightly as he leaned down towards Ben. 'If you dare,' he whispered.

Knight guessed that Ben had already met the other children, even if only briefly. The three of them were sitting in the lecture hall. Gemma and Rupam sat in the front row of the large amphitheatre-like room. Maria was near the back, scowling down at the rows of empty seats as they listened to the lesson.

Knight led Ben in through a door at the back of the hall. He looked down on to the semicircular stage below, where an elderly lady was standing at a wooden lectern. She leaned heavily on a walking stick as she peered through horn-rimmed glasses at a bundle of notes in front of her. She had white hair that stood out in a mass of curls round her head like a halo. She was wearing a tweed skirt and a dark knitted cardigan.

'So the events at Widdecombe Hall would seem to bear out my earlier point,' she was saying, 'about the importance of checking thoroughly for curses and other enchantments that may have been placed on an area or property in antiquity.'

She looked up over the top of her glasses as Knight led Ben down towards the stage.

'Forgive me, Madam Sosostram,' Knight said. 'I've brought you a new pupil whom I'd like to introduce to everyone.'

Ben stood nervously beside Knight. Gemma and Rupam smiled at him. Maria turned away, sitting sideways on her chair.

'I'm sure you've met already,' Knight announced, 'but this is Ben Foundling. He'll be joining you for the time being. Maria . . .'

Maria swung slowly round to glare down at them.

'Maria, I'm sure you and the others will make Ben very welcome. It's all a bit new to him.' Knight turned to Ben. 'Maria has been my Personal Seer for a long time. For the last eighteen months she's been helping to train Gemma to take over.'

Maria's scowl deepened and she looked away again.

'Gemma you met briefly at the home,' Knight went on. 'And finally, Rupam is one of our star pupils. He's still here because it's too far for him to go home between terms. Partly, anyway. Our terms don't match with the normal school terms,' he added.

Rupam gave Ben a wave and mouthed, 'Hi.'

'You can speak more over lunch. For now, I think it will do Ben good to sit in on your session, Madam Sosostram, if that's all right. After lunch, he'll be joining Gemma and myself.'

The old lady nodded. 'He will be most welcome.'

Knight patted Ben reassuringly on the shoulder before leaving by a door at the back of the stage area.

'You can sit at the front here with the children who are willing and ready to learn,' Madam Sosostram told Ben. 'Or,' she added, her glasses twinkling in the light as she turned, 'you can sit at the back with those who mistakenly think they know everything.'

Ben looked up at Maria, who was inspecting her fingernails.

'I'll sit with Gemma and Rupam,' he said.

Madam Sosostram smiled. 'I think you're going to get on very well here, Ben. Welcome to the School of Night. Our subject for today is contemporary witchcraft . . .'

11

IT WAS GETTING DARK AND THE MIST CLUNG TO the ground as if it was seeping out of the earth itself. Tombstones emerged from the grey as if they were floating in the mist. The church was a dark pencil sketch, vague and insubstantial. It was strange to find such a place in the middle of a modern city. Tower blocks of concrete and glass rose up either side of the cemetery. Monuments of a very different kind.

There wasn't room for three of them in Knight's Morgan, so they'd come in a modern saloon car. Ben sat in the back with Gemma. Gemma spent the journey staring out of the window and biting her bottom lip.

'Nervous?' Ben whispered after over an hour.

Gemma forced a thin smile. 'Always. Schools are OK – just children and the Judgement Box. But a mission . . .' She turned back to the window.

'So where are we heading? What are we going to do?'

She shrugged. 'Dunno.'

Ben looked at Knight and found the man was watching him in the rear-view mirror as he drove.

'I like to get Gemma's first impressions,' he said. 'That's why I don't give her the details. We're nearly there.'

Standing by the car at the gate into the graveyard, Ben knew what his own first impressions were. 'Spooky,' he said.

'That's the point,' Gemma told him.

'Gemma, you come with me and we'll see if we can work out what's going on.' Knight raised a finger to Ben to stop him following. 'You can wait here for the Reverend.'

Ben watched the two of them make their cautious way into the graveyard. Soon they were swallowed up by the gathering mist.

'Ben Foundling!' The voice was deep and gruff, right behind Ben.

He gave a yelp of surprise and whirled round.

A dark-cloaked figure stood beside the car. A hood covered the figure's head so that its face was wreathed in darkness.

'Are you a ghost?' Ben stammered, taking a step backwards.

The figure advanced towards him. It raised a pale hand and pushed back the hood of the cloak. 'Good gracious me, no.' Beneath the hood was a very ordinary-looking man with a round, ruddy face. 'I am the Reverend Alistair Growl. Mr Knight called me to say he was bringing a new chap with him. That must be you. How do you do?'

Relieved, but with his heart still pounding, Ben shook hands with the man. Beneath the cloak, he saw that Growl was wearing a black cassock and clerical collar.

'Gone to take a look, has he?' Growl asked.

'Yes. With Gemma.'

'Good, good.' Growl stared off into the misty evening. 'She's nothing too complicated. A couple of well-chosen prayers should see her off.'

'Gemma?' Ben asked, confused.

'The Grave Lady. That's what the locals call her anyway. She's been sighted on and off since the seventeenth century, according to the parish records and local gossip. But she's become a bit more of a nuisance recently. Appearing more often, frightening people. Walking through the walls of the offices over there.' He gestured to the vague shape of an office block. 'The head of the accountancy department is in hospital, you know

– weak heart, poor chap. Can't have that. Oh dear me, no, no, no.'

They stood together, staring into the deepening fog.

'Are you one of the School of Night?' Ben asked at last.

'I am indeed, for my sins. I don't know that I have a title as such, but I am a sort of visiting teacher of exorcism. I'm looking forward to teaching you, Ben.'

'Mr Knight told you about me?'

'A little. Did he tell you about himself?'

'Himself?'

Growl nodded. 'I thought not. You know, a little honesty and openness can go a long way. Knight used to see things, as I think you do now.'

Ben didn't correct him. 'You mean, like ghosts and stuff?'

'I mean like ghosts and stuff,' Growl agreed, amused. 'Oh, Dirk Knight doesn't see ghosts any more. But he used to, when he was a child. So he knows how terrible, how malevolent, some of them can be. Not our Grave Lady, she's strictly an amateur compared to some. But there are ancient powers, monstrous creatures, ghosts and demons struggling to break free and wreak havoc.'

'What happened? Why doesn't he see them now?'

'He grew out of it, just as everyone does. Well, almost everyone. I have a certain . . . facility,' he admitted. 'Though it comes at a price.'

Before Ben could ask what he meant by this, Growl went on, 'Knight lost the Sight in his early twenties. Until then he fought the darkness and he banished the spectres. But then his abilities deserted him.' Growl raised his hands in a 'what can you do?' gesture. 'He grew up. Occupational hazard, I suppose.'

'I suppose.'

'But he knows that children – some children – have an affinity with the unnatural and paranormal. It's a rare gift in a child. Even rarer for the child to retain that gift into adulthood.'

'And so now he trains those who still have it,' Ben said, remembering what Knight had told him earlier.

'He has dedicated his life to learning all he can about the ghosts and demons, creatures and spectres. No one alive knows more than Dirk Knight. No one alive is better qualified to arrange the exorcism of the malevolent forces. If only he can find them.' Growl put his hands on Ben's shoulders and stared deep into his eyes. 'If only he can track them down. If only he can *see* them. So that's why he trains children with the Sight to be his eyes. He trains them to seek out and exorcise the demons and spectres.'

'Yes, he told me a bit about that.'

'So now you know,' Growl said. 'There seem to be more of the unquiet and undead than ever these days. The authorities have finally come to realise that it's Dirk Knight they need to call in when there's a problem. A haunted office block, a possessed cat, or –' he turned to gesture at the misty landscape – 'sightings in a graveyard. Whatever it is, the police, the army, even the museums and the physicians discreetly send for Dirk Knight.' He leaned forward so that his round face was all that Ben could see. 'Are you sure you're ready to go with him?'

Ben wasn't sure at all, but before he could answer Growl straightened up again. 'Not a word,' he whispered to Ben. 'I only just got here, all right?'

As he spoke, the dark shapes of Knight and Gemma materialised out of the mist in front of them.

Gemma looked happier and Ben guessed that she was less nervous now she knew what they were facing.

'You know what's going on?' Knight said to Growl as they shook hands.

'Oh indeed, yes, yes, yes. Seems straightforward enough. I really didn't need you to come all this way.'

Knight nodded. 'A poor restless soul who craves sleep. Gemma could see her easily enough just now. I'm sure you can manage very well on your own.'

'But there do seem to be a lot of them about,' Growl said seriously.

'Something drawing them out, you think?'

Growl nodded. 'Possibly. What do you think, Gemma?'

'There's more of everything,' she said. 'I see more every time I come out. Maybe there's no room left in Heaven and Hell.'

No one seemed to want to speculate on that suggestion. After an awkward pause, Knight said, 'Right, let's get this over with, then. We can talk afterwards about . . . other things. You sure you're up to this, Alistair?'

The clergyman sighed and nodded. 'Did she die violently? *It* seems more drawn to the violent deaths.'

Ben wanted to ask Growl what he meant, but a warning glance from Knight silenced him.

'Plague,' Gemma said. 'She caught it from her brother. He lived, but she died. I could see the resentment and the bitterness. And the sweat from the fever on her face.'

'Ladies don't sweat,' Growl said quietly. 'That's for men and horses. Ladies perspire.'

They had started walking, following Gemma deep into the graveyard. The girl was looking round constantly, staring into the misty distance.

'She'll be here again soon. I can feel the chill of her coming.'

The mist seemed to swirl, as if a large shape was pushing through and blowing it aside. But Ben couldn't see anything.

'There she is,' Gemma said, pointing.

'I can see her,' Growl said. His voice seemed even deeper, gruffer and less friendly.

'Will she manifest?' Knight asked. 'The locals have seen her, so she must become tangible, surely. Can you see her, Ben?'

As he spoke, the gap in the mist seemed to solidify into a shape. A woman. Ben had expected her to be old and hunched. But she was young, walking upright, carrying a small bunch of withered flowers.

'Yes – yes, I can,' Ben said, his voice husky with fear.

Knight nodded. 'Me too. A complete manifestation. Anyone else watching will get a shock – she's come right through into the real world. A proper ghost, if you will.'

The young woman's face was as pale as her dress and her expression was completely blank, stony as a statue. She looked at Ben as she approached. He thought that actually she had a kindly face – innocent and unblemished.

Then the face changed. In a moment it was a snarling mask of rage and fury. The mouth opened impossibly wide and the woman howled. It was a noise filled with anger and despair, loathing and hatred. Her fingers stretched out like talons as she hurled herself at Ben and the others.

'Time you were going,' Growl said, stepping in front of the shrieking woman.

'Are you sure . . .' Ben started. Despite his fear, he didn't like the idea of leaving the kindly old man with this creature.

Growl turned and his transformation was every bit as extreme as the woman's. His face was twisted in anger. 'Just go!' he roared. 'Leave us!'

'Us?'

Gemma grabbed Ben's arm. 'Leave him,' she said. 'He can manage.'

Ben stumbled after Gemma, with Knight following close behind. He glanced back and through the mist he saw the Reverend Alistair Growl raise his hand, like a monk giving a blessing.

He could see the old man's lips moving, though he couldn't hear what he was saying. The air was filled with the cries and screams of the ghostly woman as she twisted and writhed and clawed the air.

The air seemed to explode, exactly where the woman had been. The mist closed round the figure of Growl and then there was silence.

They waited for about ten minutes by the car before Growl joined them. His cloak was caked in mud and he looked exhausted.

'Well,' he said, 'I think that's all sorted out now.' He beamed at Ben, as if his earlier angry outburst had never happened. 'You'd best go and check,' he said to Gemma. 'Just to be on the safe side. Your sensitivities are so much better tuned than mine.'

'Go with her, Ben,' Knight said. He helped Growl to the car, opening the door so the old man could sit inside.

Ben followed Gemma back into the graveyard. 'Has she gone?'

'Oh yes,' Gemma said. She too seemed to be back to her normal, carefree self. 'Growl just wants a minute alone with Mr Knight.'

'Why?'

Gemma grinned. 'Probably to talk about you.'

'Oh, thanks . . . Really?'

'I don't know, do I? But Mr Knight wanted to talk to Growl.'

'So what was wrong with him?' Ben asked. 'Why did he get so angry?'

'You didn't do as he asked.' She was serious again now as she turned to look at him. 'You mustn't upset the Reverend when he's working.' More than serious, she sounded scared. 'Never upset him. Not ever.'

Seeing Ben's worried expression, Gemma's own softened. She took his hand. 'You've got loads to learn. It'll be such fun. I'm glad you're here. Come on.'

She led him back through the misty graveyard, forever looking from side to side. Ben could sense that she was seeing the spirits of the dead at every step. He could see nothing himself, nothing out of the ordinary. But he shuddered at the sight of the glistening tombstones sweating in the mist. *Fun* was not the word he would have chosen.

12

IN THE MIDDLE OF THE NIGHT, BEN WOKE WITH the horrifying face of the screaming woman imprinted on his dreams. The duvet had slipped off the bed and he lay for a while shivering and listening to the moaning of the wind outside. The windows rattled and rain scattered across them.

He pulled the duvet back on to the bed and snuggled underneath it. Knight had told Ben that tomorrow he would start his education. Mrs Bailey would set him English and maths and 'ordinary' schoolwork. But alongside that, he would have other lessons and lectures. Ben was conscious that his life had changed. He hoped it would be for the better.

He hoped it would help him discover what had happened to Sam.

But how much would Knight help – how much *could* he help? Tired and confused, Ben drifted back into sleep.

In the event, Knight had already left by the time Ben joined the other children for breakfast the following morning. Over the next few days, Knight was hardly at the house. Sometimes Gemma went with him and once he took Maria as well. But usually he went on his own.

'He's a busy man,' Mrs Bailey told Ben. 'You were lucky he was here when you arrived. More often than not he's away on business. But he has arranged for you to stay with us here. That's all sorted out officially now.'

The lessons with Mrs Bailey were similar to others Ben had had at a variety of different schools. But now it was just him with Rupam and Gemma. Maria rarely joined them, but Ben saw her sometimes out on the lawn with Mrs Bailey, training in martial arts or with a sword. Maria's sword strokes were practised and elegant. But however fast she moved, Mrs Bailey's sword was always faster. It was as if she could anticipate every move that Maria made before it actually happened.

Ben, Rupam and Gemma had workbooks rather than swords and Mrs Bailey spent time with each of them in turn. Ben was about to ask her if she was really a teacher when she told him she was actually trained as one. 'A long time ago,' she added, smiling. Though Ben didn't think she looked that old.

Interspersed with Mrs Bailey's lessons, Ben learned about the world he could not see – ghosts and spirits, demons and other creatures. Some of the sessions were in the lecture hall where he'd first met Madam Sosostram. Others were in a small classroom with a video camera recording whoever was in charge of the lesson.

'There's a special website,' Rupam told Ben, 'where students can view the lessons. Some of the School of Night sessions are actually video-linked in real time to other places too.'

'Like where?' Ben wondered.

'After-school clubs, youth centres,' Gemma said. 'All over.'

'It's stored on DVD,' Maria said. 'You can watch any lesson again if you need to.' She didn't make it sound as if this was something she wanted to do herself. 'Just ask Webby and he'll set it up.'

'Who?'

The Reverend Alistair Growl, who was running

this session, cleared his throat and raised his eyebrows for silence. There was no hint at the angry temper he'd briefly displayed in the churchyard, however, and soon he was enthusiastically explaining the finer details of different types of exorcism and when to use them.

Having lessons with Rupam was both amusing and frustrating. He seemed to absorb the information immediately and he remembered *everything*. Everything he read, everything anyone said – he could replay it as if he was reading or hearing it again.

When Ben couldn't tell Growl the gist of the particular type of exorcism he'd just explained, the clergyman sighed and asked Rupam, 'What did I just say?'

Rupam didn't look up from his work. But he recited the whole speech Growl had just delivered. Word perfect. Then he looked up and grinned at Ben. 'Easy. Don't know what it means though,' he added.

'How does he do that?' Ben whispered to Gemma as Growl continued.

'Rupam can remember anything,' Gemma said quietly.

'He'll remind you of your most embarrassing

moments at the most embarrassing time,' Maria whispered from across the table.

Growl clapped his hands together for silence. 'Children,' he chided, 'this is actually important. It could save your life. Or your soul. Now, Ben, can you tell me why bell, book and candle are so powerful when used together for exorcism?'

Ben couldn't. But Rupam knew.

Only Mrs Bailey – and Knight, when he was there – lived at the house with the children. Ben assumed that the groundsman, Pendleton Jones, whom he'd met when he first arrived must live close by.

Occasionally he met the man outside when he went for a walk. The children were all under strict instructions not to leave the grounds of Gibbet Manor without permission. Remembering his narrow escape from the shadowy creature when he arrived at the gates that first evening, Ben was happy to heed the warning.

It wasn't Pendleton Jones whom Ben looked for outside in the grounds. It was Sam. He hoped she would turn up again, though he didn't really expect it. More and more he wondered if he'd imagined meeting her by the lake.

Ben helped Pendleton Jones set spirit traps near the outer wall. They were small boxes made from polished wood with a pentagram of mother of pearl inlaid in the lid. One side of the box was a dark wire mesh.

'It's like a mousetrap,' Jones explained. 'The spirit can get through the mesh to see what's inside. It can smell the wood, which has been smoked with incense to attract it. But once it's in, a powerful binding force holds it there and it can't dissipate enough to get through the mesh and escape.'

'Then what do you do?' Ben asked.

'Depends. If it's harmless, just a sprite, then I take it out of the grounds and release it.'

'And if it's dangerous?'

'If it falls into the trap, then I seal the box in wax and bury it. But the more dangerous ones tend to be more clever too. They can sense the traps and avoid them. You need to take drastic action to keep them out, if they ever come looking.'

'I should be getting back,' Ben said as they set the last of the spirit traps. 'I've got a lesson with Madam Sosostram this afternoon.'

'Virginia Gibbs,' Jones said, nodding.

'What?'

'Madam Sosostram is the most accomplished

witch in the south of England. Maybe in the whole of Britain. But her real name is Virginia Gibbs. Better not let on that I told you, though. In fact,' Jones continued as they walked back to the small hut where he stored his tools and traps, 'better not tell any of them you've spoken to me. They'll only worry what I might have told you about them. It can be our secret, all right?'

Ben was late for the session with Madam Sosostram. He slipped into the back of the lecture hall and sat close to Maria, who was scowling as usual. She didn't say much and when she did it was usually snappy or terse.

'She'll get over it,' Rupam had once told Ben.

'No, she won't,' Gemma had told them both.

Maria glanced up at Ben as he sat down and there was the barest trace of a smile of greeting. He grinned back at her and she looked away.

'As I was saying . . .' Madam Sosostram said loudly, banging her stick on the floor and staring up at Ben as she spoke. 'The last witchcraft act in Britain wasn't repealed until the middle of the twentieth century. There is still a stigma attached, an underlying suspicion of the supernatural. Oh, many people are happy to read their horoscopes and some even believe what they read. But there's an assumption – a flawed assumption – that there must be some sort of scientific rather than magical basis for predicting the future with charts and star maps.'

She gave a little snort of what might have been outrage. Her spectacles, dangling on a silver chain round her neck, bounced on her chest in sympathy.

'Might as well consult the entrails of a goat,' she went on. 'To understand astrology, alchemy and the other arts we must acknowledge that they are based on a science that the modern world no longer understands or accepts . . .'

Rupam and Gemma were laughing together as they left the lecture hall, imagining Madam Sosostram stirring a goat's entrails in a large cooking pot. Ben paused outside the door, trying to get straight in his mind some of the things Madam Sosostram had been talking about.

'Did you get the homework?' Maria asked, following him out.

'Homework?'

'Thought not. Madame Sosostram handed it out at the beginning of the session. Worksheets.' Maria pulled a photocopied sheet from her notebook and flashed it at Ben. 'Boring or what? But you'd better go back and get one. Apologise for being late at the same time,' Maria added. 'She'll appreciate that.'

'Thanks,' Ben said. But Maria had already turned away.

Ben went back into the lecture hall. It was empty. He'd missed her – Madam Sosostram had already gone. So he hurried down the aisle past the rows of seats and out of the door at the back of the stage.

There was still no sign of Madam Sosostram. He ran down the corridor, knowing it led past the drawing room and back to the main hallway. As he turned a corner, he saw a figure ahead of him.

But it wasn't the ample and elderly form of Madam Sosostram. It was a young woman with long blonde hair. She seemed to sense that Ben was watching her and turned. Her hair spun, catching the light. Ben almost gasped out loud when he saw her face, she was so beautiful. When she smiled at him, he couldn't help but grin back.

Then the woman walked on down the corridor. She reached another corner, pausing to glance back at Ben through cat-like emerald eyes.

Ben ran after her. He turned the corner – and the corridor ahead was empty. He stopped, confused, and found himself standing outside the drawing-room door. She must have gone inside. Perhaps she would know where Madam Sosostram was.

The fire was burning lazily. A figure sat in one of the armchairs facing it. She turned as Ben entered the room, looking round the wing of the chair.

'Hello, Ben,' Madam Sosostram said.

Ben frowned. 'Are you . . . Did someone . . . I thought I saw . . .' he stammered.

'I'm sorry, did you want something? My hearing's not what it was, I'm afraid.'

Ben shook his head, confused. The young woman must have hurried on down the corridor. Maybe she'd wanted to avoid him – whoever she was.

'I didn't get the homework sheet,' Ben said. 'And I wanted to apologise for being late for your class.'

Madam Sosostram smiled, her face wrinkling up like an old apple. 'That's quite all right, young man. But don't make a habit of it, will you?' She took a worksheet from the low table beside the chair and handed it to Ben. 'Was there anything else you wanted to ask me?'

Ben assumed she meant about the class. But there were so many things he wanted to ask he didn't know where to start. So he shook his head and hurried away.

***

The next day, Ben got his phone.

It was the first time he had seen Maria smile properly. She found Ben reading in his room late in the afternoon. Rupam had lent him a book of ghost stories by M. R. James. It was a large hardback book with black-and-white drawings – moorland, old buildings, a man lost in a garden maze. He found it quite hard going, even with the pictures.

'Captain Morton is here,' Maria said. 'He wants to see you. In the drawing room.'

'Who does?' Ben asked, putting the book down.

That was when she smiled. 'Captain Morton – come on.'

More puzzled by Maria's sudden good humour than by the thought of another mysterious visiting teacher, Ben hurried after her.

Captain Morton was not like any of the other teachers. In bearing and manner he was similar to Knight – who was standing with the Captain, talking quietly, while Gemma and Rupam sat near by. The two men were similar in height and build. But Morton was wearing army uniform. His cap was on one of the side tables.

'Ben, come and meet the Captain,' Knight said.

Maria walked with Ben, as if making sure he didn't get lost on the way across the drawing room.

'James Morton,' the soldier said. His voice was clipped and efficient. 'I guess I'm the quartermaster for Mr Knight and his associates. Delivery boy and storeman rolled into one.'

'Far more than that,' Knight said.

'Did you bring any new equipment?' Maria asked.

'Boffins at Purton Point are working flat out, but nothing at the moment. Except this.'

He took a mobile phone from his jacket pocket. It looked the same as the one Ben had seen Knight use before, only with a blue case rather than a black one. Morton handed the phone to Ben.

'Maria will show you how to use it,' Morton said. 'Star pupil, she is.'

Maria was grinning. 'I had a good teacher.'

'We all have phones like that,' Rupam announced. 'Though Gemma doesn't really need hers. Those of us who aren't so gifted find them useful.'

'What for?' Ben said. 'I mean, I can see it's a phone. But so what? Who are we going to call?'

'Ghostbusters,' Morton said.

Rupam grinned, Knight gave a wry smile and Maria actually laughed.

'Among other things, it will help you see,' Knight said. He took the phone from Ben and flipped it open. 'This operates the camera.'

He pressed a button below the main number keys. It was labelled with a simple white square. The screen lit up at once and an image appeared on it – Morton's amused face as Knight aimed the phone at him.

'There are various settings,' Morton explained. 'Infrared enhancement, digital zoom, two hours' recording time for audio and video, and five levels of psi detection.'

'Of what?'

'The phone can show things that are invisible to most human eyes,' Morton said.

'It shows something of what is happening on the ethereal plane,' Knight explained, still pointing the phone at Morton. 'Not always, but often. It will show shadows and flickers – hints of ghosts and demons, creatures and monsters, as well as the supernatural aura that often surrounds a child gifted with the Sight. Things you might not pick up even if you do have the Sight.'

Knight handed Ben the phone. 'It's set to auto-detect. Morton has no ability, any more than I do, or than you seem to – even at level 5. I guess your ability comes and goes. We need to train that, so you can call it up at will. But try Maria, Rupam and Gemma.'

Ben turned, holding the phone out in front of him and aiming it at Maria. She was still smiling, but while the rest of the picture was just what he'd expect to see on a mobile phone camera, Maria seemed to be glowing. Just slightly – as if she was lit from behind.

With Rupam the effect was similar – a glowing edge, a shimmer. An aura.

When Ben turned the phone towards Gemma, it was difficult to make out any detail she was glowing so much.

'With your sister, Sam,' Knight said quietly, 'the whole screen went white.'

13

THE CHILDREN HAD THEIR OWN PLAYROOM, though Maria called it a living room, where they could spend their free time. They tended to congregate there in the evening, lounging in the battered armchairs or on the old sofa. There were books, a TV with DVDs and games consoles, and a couple of up-to-date laptop computers with wireless Internet connections. There was also a kettle for them to make hot drinks and a fridge which Mrs Bailey kept stocked with cold drinks, healthy snacks and the occasional bar of chocolate.

It was here that Ben got to know the others. Gemma and Rupam told him more about Maria than the girl did herself. She was the oldest – eighteen according to Gemma, but Rupam said she was guessing.

'Where does she come from?' Ben wondered one lunchtime.

Neither of them knew. 'She was here before we were,' Rupam said.

'When I first came here, I thought she was Knight's daughter,' Gemma confessed.

Rupam laughed.

'It's not that funny.'

'Just can't imagine Knight having children,' Rupam said.

'Except us,' Ben pointed out.

Rupam's smile faded. 'I suppose.'

He was from India, somewhere close to Mumbai. 'Different sort of spirits and demons over there,' Rupam said knowingly. 'Not better or worse, just different. My uncle could see them too, when he was younger. He's in the local government, knows some people. They contacted Knight and here I am.'

'Don't you go home between terms?' Ben asked.

Rupam frowned. 'Why would I do that? I remember everything about home. Every detail. Every moment I lived there.' He shuddered. 'I have no wish to go back.'

Ben knew better than to ask any more. Instead he asked Gemma if she had family.

'I'm like you, Ben. A *foundling*, with no parents. I was living with my nan when Mr Knight came to our school. I thought he was funny – with his box and Maria . . .' She stared off into the distance, remembering. 'Until he opened the box. Maria used to laugh and smile back then. She could see as much as me.'

'But not now?'

'She sees less than she used to,' Rupam said.

Then Maria came in to get herself a cup of tea, and Ben and the others moved on to computer games.

Ben and Rupam played a battle game with futuristic tanks attacking robot soldiers dug in round a ruined city. Gemma was happy to sit and watch – clapping when things went well and sighing loudly when they didn't. She seemed even more involved than Ben and Rupam.

Two levels of game-play later and they were stuck. Rupam's tank was bogged down in a muddy street, surrounded by rubble. Ben's was between a collapsed bridge and a huge bomb crater. After several attempts to drive over the rubble or move fast enough to make it over the gap in the bridge, both of them were ready to give up.

'It's impossible,' Ben complained.

'There must be a way to do it,' Rupam said.

'But what is it?'

'I don't know.'

'Webby will know,' Gemma said. 'I bet Webby knows. Let's ask him. He won't mind.'

'I suppose,' Rupam said glumly. 'Though we should be able to work it out ourselves.'

'Who's Webby?' Ben wanted to know. He'd heard the name mentioned before.

'You haven't met Webby?' Rupam's mood immediately brightened. 'You must meet Webby.'

Maria looked up from her cup of tea and a paperback romance. 'Don't eat the pizza,' she warned. 'It's growing things.'

Heading the other way past the lecture hall, they came to a door at the end of the corridor. It was opened by a number pad – the code was 666. Beyond the door, stone steps disappeared into the gloom.

'There's lights on at the bottom,' Rupam told Ben. 'You'll see as soon as we turn the corner.'

'Unless Webby's asleep,' Gemma added.

Rupam laughed. 'Webby doesn't sleep.'

'So who is Webby?' Ben asked as he followed Rupam down the stairs.

'He's just . . . Webby. He runs the website, works all the computers and everything.'

'And he does it from the cellar.'

'The vault,' Gemma corrected him.

The light did indeed increase as soon as Ben was round the corner of the stairs. And he felt the cold, like walking into a fridge. There was a noise too – a steady thump like a heartbeat.

The cellar was a single large room with whitewashed brick walls. A big arched alcove at one end held a wine rack full of dusty bottles. A circular metal door like you might find on a submarine filled another alcove. A heavy locking wheel was fixed in the middle and huge bolts held the door in place.

'The vault is actually through there,' Rupam told Ben. 'It's like a big safe or strongroom.'

'So what's in the vault?'

Rupam shrugged. 'No idea. Never been inside.'

Most of the rest of the cellar was taken up with computer equipment – system boxes, monitor screens, disk drives. Cables ran across the floor like creepers and up the walls like vines.

In among the jungle of wires and cables was a narrow bed, on top of which was a cardboard box with a pizza in it. Ben didn't need to look too closely to know that Maria had been right – not everything on the pizza was original topping; some of it had grown since. A couple of slices had been pulled away, but they didn't look like they had been touched any more than the rest of the pizza.

In the middle of it all sat a young man in a wheeled office chair. He had long, dark, greasy hair and was wearing jeans and a denim shirt. He looked incredibly pale and rather gaunt, with angular features and dark-rimmed eyes. The heartbeat thump of rhythm was coming from his earphones, connected to one of the computers in front of him.

'That's Webby,' Gemma said.

The man was bobbing his head in time with the music. He tapped at a keyboard, moved a mouse, slapped the side of a screen and sighed. When he saw them, he swung round rapidly in the chair, the wire from his earphones knocking a couple of CDs to the floor, but he didn't seem to notice.

'Hi, guys,' Webby said – more loudly than was necessary. 'Hang on.' He pulled out the earphones and clicked with his mouse, stopping the beat of the music. 'What can I do you for?'

'We came to introduce Ben,' Rupam said. 'He's new.'

'Hi there, new Ben,' Webby said. 'Look, will this take long, only I want to finish up here. Just another week or two and I'm out of here.'

‘He’s always saying that,’ Gemma whispered to Ben.

‘So what do you do down here?’ Ben asked. ‘Is this where you live?’

Webby picked up a can of coke from one of the worktops. He swilled it round, then put it down again without drinking.

‘Just till the job’s done,’ Webby said. ‘Taking a bit longer than expected. But as soon as everything’s set up and working properly, I’m history.’ He pointed to the main screen in front of him. ‘Monitoring the various emails, text messages and reports that come in from the School of Night agents out in the field. That’s the other kids to you, Ben.’

‘Webby set up all the systems,’ Rupam explained. ‘Any agent can report in, then Webby’s systems automatically filter out the important information and pass it on so Mr Knight can decide what to do about it. Isn’t that right?’

‘Sure is,’ Webby agreed. ‘Every time one of you guys uses their mobile, the image data is sent here to be analysed and stored. It’s a full-time job keeping all the systems running and monitoring all the messages and reports that come in. Then there’s the blogs and the conspiracy websites that I need to keep checking for any hint of dangerous paranormal activity that might need further investigation. You can only automate so much of it.'

'Keeps you busy, then,' Ben said.

'Oh, I'm just doing it until the systems are all up and running properly. Short-term contract, you see. Not a lifetime's work. Can't wait to move on to the next challenge. That's what it's all about. Variety – the spice of life.'

Gemma nudged Rupam to ask about the tank battle game and Webby laughed.

'You're supposed to pick up anti-gravity converters from the warehouse on the previous level once you clear it of bad guys. Then you fit those to your tanks using the upgrade option and float out of the rubble and over the bridge. Easy.'

Rupam looked at Ben and shook his head. 'Oh yes, easy. We should have guessed.'

'Thanks,' Ben said.

'Any time.' Webby pushed his earphones back in and started the music again. 'Catch me while you can, though,' he shouted above the noise in his ears. 'Shan't be here much longer.'

'When does he leave?' Ben asked as they climbed back up the stairs.

'Never,' Rupam said. 'He says he's on a three-month contract.'

'He's been here longer than any of us,' Gemma said. 'Except maybe Maria.'

Rupam nodded. 'He's been here for years. I think he likes it down there. He never goes out.'

'So does he sleep down there?' Ben asked. 'I saw he had a bed.'

They had reached the top of the stairs. Knight was standing waiting for them in the corridor.

'Maria told me you were down here,' he said.

'Sorry,' Ben said instinctively. He assumed they were about to be told off.

'Oh, it's no problem.' Knight smiled. 'I'm sure it does Webby good to see some real people now and again, rather than just his machines.' He turned to Gemma. 'It's time we were going. Are you ready?'

Gemma nodded. 'Sorry, I'd forgotten the time. I'll get my coat.'

'No problem, but we need to make a start.' He turned to go, then changed his mind and turned back. 'We're off to a school about fifty miles away,' he said to Ben. 'One of the teachers there is a former pupil of the School of Night and she thinks she's got a few children who might be of interest. Why don't you come along as well and keep Gemma company? You never know,' he added as he headed off down the corridor, 'you might learn something.'

Miss Jansis had asked some children to stay back after school for a reading club. There were half a dozen nine- and ten-year-olds in a temporary classroom that was parked like a large caravan in the playground of Tollarton Hall Primary School.

It was like a replay of the special assembly at the home, but in less impressive surroundings and with fewer, younger children. Knight didn't bother to send any children out, there were so few to start with. Gemma sat at the side of the classroom, watching the six children intently. Ben sat beside her while Knight set up his Judgement Box on the teacher's desk. The children watched with interest.

'We've been reading about pirates and treasure, haven't we?' Miss Jansis said. She was a small lady, with tiny glasses and a northern accent. 'Can you guess what our visitor has in his box?'

'I bet it's treasure,' one boy said.

'Or an elephant,' a girl suggested.

'An elephant would be too big,' the boy told her.

'Not if it's a baby elephant.'

Knight unlocked the box. Again he murmured the words that Ben had half heard in his study.

'What's he doing?' Ben asked Gemma.

'You know what's in there. The box is like a gateway to part of Hell. You have to know the right words of power to open it. And to close it again. To seal it tight shut so nothing can escape from it.' Gemma leaned closer to Ben. 'Can you see it? Her aura?' she asked quietly.

'Of course.' Though Ben couldn't see anything. He didn't even know which girl Gemma was talking about. He took out his mobile phone and flipped it open.

At once he knew who Gemma meant. She was sitting beside the elephant girl and on the phone it looked as if her hair was on fire. Knight glanced across at Gemma and Ben. Gemma nodded, indicating the girl with the aura.

Then Knight opened the box.

'No elephant, I'm afraid,' he said, tipping the box so the children could see inside. 'No treasure either. In fact – can any of you see anything at all?' He was staring at the girl with the aura, looking to see her reaction.

She went white, her mouth trembling.

Quickly, Knight closed the lid of the box. He

locked it and spoke quietly again: *'Arceo excludum coerceo Hades terminus.'*

Miss Jansis hurried to the girl. 'Oh dear, Toni – are you all right? It was just a box. I expect you're tired. Have you had a drink recently?'

But Ben heard none of the fussing. He barely noticed Knight talking quietly to Gemma, then taking Miss Jansis to one side to give instructions for monitoring the girl's progress and gradually introducing her to the world of ghosts and demons . . .

Ben was staring ashen-faced at the screen of his mobile phone. He was biting back the urge to yell out in fright and disgust. On the phone, for the first time, he had seen what was really inside the Judgement Box.

He knew from talking to Gemma that the more gifted children might see the vague shape of the creature. They might see shadows and flickering images. Glimpses of the thing that lived in the box.

What Ben had seen on his phone was much, much clearer – much, much worse. He could only begin to guess what Gemma might be able to see. What Sam had seen. The fleeting image that Ben had witnessed was more than enough.

An imp of a creature with skin like the bark of an old tree. A forked tail, gleaming yellow eyes, a forked tongue that licked over drawn-back lips. Teeth as sharp as blades. A face so ugly and horrific that Ben never ever wanted to see anything like it again.

'I need some fresh air,' he gasped to Gemma and Knight, and left them to finish with Miss Jansis while the children chose their reading books.

There was a woman standing by the school gate. Probably a mum come to collect her child from the reading group, Ben thought. Except she didn't look like he'd expect a school mum to look. She was about the right age to have a ten-year-old child, but she was dressed smartly in a dark jacket and skirt, her black hair falling in perfect symmetry round her face and on to her shoulders. She was holding a briefcase. Perhaps she'd come straight from work.

But if she was a waiting mum, why didn't she come into the playground? She was standing on the other side of the school fence and she was looking over at the temporary classroom that Ben had just left. Was she a teacher?

The woman's head moved, tracking from the classroom to the gate in the fence. It was an odd movement – as if she was watching someone walk quickly across the playground. Only there was no one there.

Just a woman waiting outside the school gates. Ben was unsettled by the sight of the creature in the Judgement Box. He was seeing mysteries and secrets everywhere. He realised he was still holding his phone and made to close it up and put it away.

As he moved, the image on the screen showed the playground. It showed the woman beyond the fence. It showed the playground gate, where she was now looking. It showed a hunched, leathery creature that scuttled out of the gate and up to the woman.

It was about thirty centimetres tall and looked as if it was made of stone. The creature had claws for hands and feet and it moved like a monkey, knuckles grazing the ground. A pair of jagged wings, translucent skin stretched like parchment between spikes of bone, was folded across its back. It had the face of a grinning gargoyle and Ben knew that it had been hiding outside the classroom – watching and listening.

The woman bent down slightly and the creature leapt up on to her shoulder. It perched there, like a bizarre and terrifying pirate's parrot, as the woman turned and walked away.

Looking up from the image on his phone, unable to see what was sitting on the woman's shoulder, Ben saw that she was walking awkwardly to compensate for the creature's weight. She walked with one shoulder slightly stooped, lopsided, ungainly . . . Just like the thin man Ben had seen at the home the night Miss Haining was attacked. And now he knew what had attacked her.

'Are you all right?' Knight asked, smiling down at Ben. 'You look like you've just seen a ghost.'

14

NIGHT'S EXPRESSION BECAME MORE GRAVE as he listened to Ben's story.

'You saw it on your phone?' Gemma asked.

Ben nodded. He didn't want to admit he couldn't see the creature except with his phone, so he said, 'I wanted to check, to be sure there was something there.'

'Did *you* see anything, sense anything?' Knight asked Gemma.

'There was something,' she admitted. 'Just a feeling. But I was concentrating on the classroom, not the playground outside, or who might be looking in. I thought it was the imp in the Judgement Box I could sense. Didn't see anything, though.'

'You didn't want to,' Ben told her, shuddering at the memory of the creature. Even as he said it, he realised that Gemma probably saw more frightening things every day.

'Back to the car,' Knight decided. 'The woman you saw will be far away by now. But we'll call Webby. He can analyse the images and data from your phone. If he isn't on it already.'

It was getting dark as they drove back to Gibbet Manor. Knight called Webby, who had indeed already noticed the paranormal activity detected by Ben's phone.

His voice sounded slightly hollow coming from the speakers in the car: 'I assumed he was looking at the imp in the box. But I did double-check. It's been a quiet afternoon. Like all the demons have gone on holiday for a bit.'

'Not very likely,' Knight told him.

'Anyway, I'm analysing it now. Running a search on our lady with the Grotesque. Should be done by the time you get back.'

'Grotesque?' Ben asked, after Knight had ended the call.

'Just what we call them,' Gemma said.

'Like a witch's familiar,' Knight explained. 'A Grotesque is a small demon or spirit that works for a particular human, or occasionally a group of people who act together. It's bound to them by words of power and has to obey their will and do their bidding.'

'Imp-slave,' Ben said.

'Sort of. They never stray far from their human master or mistress. The two are bound together by an invisible thread, if you like. They become different aspects of the same person. So even though the adult probably doesn't have the Sight as such, they can see the Grotesque.'

'It's very rare,' Gemma added. 'Not many people are clever enough to know how to bind a demon to them. And not many of them are powerful enough to be able to do it.'

'But we are coming across more of this sort of thing,' Knight said grimly.

'Me too,' Ben muttered.

Knight turned to look at Ben over his shoulder. Just a glance, then he was concentrating on the road ahead again. 'What do you mean?'

Ben's mouth was dry. His stomach lurched like it did when he got travel-sick. But that wasn't the problem now. He should tell Knight, he decided. It could be important – and it might be a vital clue to what had happened to Sam.

'After my sister disappeared,' he said, 'there was a man. He walked awkwardly, with his shoulder bent under an invisible weight. I didn't see it, but I heard it laughing – his Grotesque. It attacked Miss Haining, drove her mad.'

'Mr Magill told me about that. He didn't mention any man. Who was he? What did he look like?'

'It was dark. I didn't really see him properly. Tall and very thin, with fair hair. He walked kind of lopsided.'

Knight's eyes watched Ben carefully in the rear-view mirror for several seconds. 'Maybe Webby can find a connection,' he said. 'Tell me everything that happened, all you can remember. Absolutely everything.'

The cellar was crowded enough with all Webby's equipment. Now with Knight, Gemma, Ben, Maria, Rupam and Mrs Bailey also present, there was hardly room to stand, though it still felt incredibly cold.

The only space was between the sets of monitors where Webby wheeled his office chair at speed between keyboards, tapping away on several different search engines and databases at once.

A screen at one end of his L-shaped arrangement of desks showed what looked like a weather map of the British Isles, with areas shaded in different colours. Another showed a still image taken from the recording Ben's phone had automatically made and sent in. Webby zoomed in on it so that the woman with black hair was frozen in position, staring out of the screen. On the monitor next to it, a succession of female faces flashed up in a window.

'No match yet,' Webby reported. 'Must be quite a powerful lady, though.'

'To control a Grotesque of that magnitude, you mean?' Knight said.

'No, I mean to afford a jacket like that. I've cross-referenced CCTV at the only stores that sell it. Nothing so far.'

'Perhaps someone bought it for her,' Maria suggested. There was a hint of envy in her tone.

'Or maybe she nicked it,' Ben said.

Gemma and Rupam grinned, but no one else reacted to the comment.

'Look,' Mrs Bailey said, pointing at the screen sorting through the different women.

It seemed to Ben that she spoke before the flashing images stopped, displaying a grainy photograph of the same woman.

'That's her,' Ben agreed.

Webby leapt up from his chair and rattled at the keyboard. A mass of data scrolled up next to the picture of the woman. Other images appeared too – a profile shot, a scanned reproduction of a newspaper article, a collection of tiny faces headed 'Known Associates' . . .

'Daniella Lawton,' Webby announced. 'Thirty-two years old. Inherited her father's company, which manufactures electrical components. Floated it on the stock market and made out like a bandit. She's worth millions and she wants even more. Ambitious is an understatement. House in London, bigger house in Kent. Holiday cottage in Portugal . . . Well, I say "cottage", but it's got a swimming pool and tennis courts. And her own jet to get there, of course.'

'Any paranormal background?' Knight asked.

'Has her own private astrologer. Been seen at seances and meetings of the European Alchemical Society. Has a stake in a research lab looking into what they call New Age solutions. Think they can cure cancer with healing stones and incantations, that sort of thing.'

'Can they?' Gemma asked.

Webby shrugged. 'Who knows. Doubt it, though, or they'd be selling it big time.'

'So what's she doing outside a primary school in the south-west of England?' Rupam asked.

'Good question,' Knight acknowledged. 'Anyone got any suggestions?'

Webby moved over to the screen with the coloured map on it. 'I asked Captain Morton if his American friends could spare us a satellite for an hour or two. There's a spirit-filter on the image, so this shows – very roughly – the levels of paranormal activity over Britain. The redder the colour, the more activity. So clusters round the major population centres, as you'd expect. All pretty normal.' He grinned. 'Or paranormal.'

'And how does that help?' Knight asked.

'Well, we should have enough historical data now to assemble a sequence of the last few hours. If we zoom in – and I have no idea if the resolution will be high enough . . .'

Webby clicked with his mouse and the image homed in on the South-West. Ben had seen similar images when he played on Google Earth. But the pictures of the houses, streets and fields were overlaid with a sprinkling of coloured dots.

'As good as it gets,' Webby decided as the image began to break up into pixellated confusion. 'But that yellow splodge there is your friendly imp in his box. And this one –' he pointed to a deep orange mark close by – 'must be Miss Daniella Lawton's personal Grotesque. So let's run the sequence through and see where it goes . . .'

The image tracked across the countryside, through several small towns. It was all a confused blur to Ben. But he could tell that the orange stain that marked the Grotesque was following the yellow indicator that represented the imp in the Judgement Box.

'She waited,' Webby said, voicing what they could all see. 'And then she followed you . . .'

The image stopped. It showed an empty expanse of green and brown, broken only by a narrow line of black – a lane leading to a large building in grounds behind a stone wall.

'She followed us here,' Knight said quietly.

'Why?' Ben asked.

Before anyone could answer, there was a loud beep from one of the computers.

'Whoa – not good,' Webby announced.

'What is it?' Rupam asked.

Webby turned a screen so they could all see. It showed a picture of a man. He was walking towards the camera, caught in mid-step. The light was behind him, so he was barely more than a silhouette against a city street. St Paul's Cathedral rose up impressively in the background.

Maria leaned closer to see the screen, her hand to her mouth as if in surprise. 'So who is he?'

'Fellow investor in the New Age lab research. And several other projects,' Webby said, reading off yet another screen. 'He's flagged in the database as a *person of interest*.'

Ben was staring at the silhouetted figure. He had recognised the man at once – the way he was walking, the dip of his left shoulder. He had seen the tall, thin man before.

'That's him – the man who was at the home. The man I was telling you about.'

'Carstairs Endeavour,' Knight said. 'I had hoped he was out of the picture after that business over ten years ago. But just recently there have been rumours . . .'

'Trouble?' Mrs Bailey asked.

'Trouble,' Knight confirmed. 'I was afraid of this.'

Maria turned away, shaking her head.

'Oh, you don't know the half of it,' Webby said.

He had turned back to the screen showing the satellite image of Gibbet Manor. Where there had been a single orange splodge close to the lane outside the main gates, there was now a swirling mass of red, like a thunderstorm on the TV weather map.

'What's going on?' Ben said. 'What does that mean?'

'I was running it on fast-forward to track the Grotesque,' Webby said. 'We can't keep the satellite link for much longer, but it's caught up with real time.' He tapped the screen with his index finger. 'That's what's happening now, right outside.'

'And red is, like, demons or spooks or Grotesques or whatever, right?' Ben said.

'Right,' Webby agreed.

Knight was staring at the screen, his expression grave. 'There must be dozens of them out there now. *That's* why the woman followed us. We led her here. She was looking for us all the time.' He straightened up and turned to Mrs Bailey. 'Get hold of Alistair Growl. Tell him we need him fast. And have Captain Morton send a containment team as quickly as possible. Let him know what's going on.'

'What *is* going on?' Gemma asked.

She seemed suddenly like a frightened little girl – it was easy for Ben to forget how young she really was. Younger than him.

'We're under siege,' Maria told her.

Knight nodded. 'Those creatures out there are preparing to attack.'

15

UP UNTIL NOW IT HAD ALL SEEMED LIKE A bizarre game. Ben had only seen the demons – and the Grotesque – on the screen of his phone. Like they were part of a computer game or a movie. Separate from the real world.

But now the tension and trepidation in the cellar made the threat seem very real. He wished he'd paid more attention to Growl in the lessons where they had been told how to banish demons and ward off malevolent spirits. Too late now.

'The grounds are protected by spirit traps,' Knight was saying. 'But only to a degree. We don't know exactly what sorts of creatures are coming, but we can't hope to keep them all out.'

'Why not?' Ben heard himself ask. He remembered Pendleton Jones setting the traps. 'Aren't we protected against them all?'

'Depends what they are,' Knight told him. 'We do have defences. But something that will keep a rat out of your house won't necessarily stop an elephant, or a wasp. Not all these creatures are the same size or power. Different types have different abilities and characteristics. The defences will keep them all out for a while, like a wall, but some will get through eventually. And we have to hold them off until Growl and Captain Morton get here.'

Maria, Rupam and Gemma seemed to know what to do. Ben followed them up to Knight's study, where Mrs Bailey was talking urgently into the phone.

Knight unlocked a cupboard at the far end of the wall. Ben got a confused glimpse of the clutter inside, but Knight pulled out several items, then closed and locked the door again.

'Safe areas, one in each room, just in case anything gets inside the house,' Knight announced. He tossed a box of chalk to Mrs Bailey. 'Standard pentagrams. You'll need to sprinkle salt round the edge of each.'

She already had her hand up, exactly positioned to catch the chalk. She hung up the phone and hurried from the room.

Knight gave Gemma an old leather-bound book.

'Spells?' Ben wondered.

'Prayers,' Rupam told him. 'In different languages and from different faiths.'

'Why not just the Lord's Prayer or something?'

'Depends what the demons believe in,' Rupam said, as if that was obvious.

He took what looked like an old lantern from Knight. Inside was a stubby yellow candle. Three of the fours sides of the lantern were mirrors, while the last was glass. Welded to the front of the lantern was an arrangement of lenses on metal rods so they could be swung away and put back in any order to focus and direct the light.

Maria was strapping on a long, thin silver sword. Knight held what looked like an ordinary handgun.

'Is that it?' Ben protested. 'What about me?'

'You're still learning,' Maria told him.

'I can help,' Ben insisted.

Knight nodded. 'Of course you can. Go to the kitchen. Get a saucepan or something and fill it from the water cooler in the corner by the sink. If you can find some way to fire it at them as they attack, so much the better. If not, just chuck it.'

'Water?' Ben said.

They were treating him like the new kid. Which, OK, he was. But he could help.

'It's holy water,' Gemma said.

The others were already hurrying from the room.

'But I've drunk from that water cooler,' Ben said.

'You're not a demon, are you?' Rupam asked, grinning despite the situation and the urgency.

'Well, no.'

'Won't do you any harm, then. I'll come with you, but get a move on.'

'Have you done this before?' Ben asked as he filled a jug and poured the water into a large cooking pot.

'Not too full,' Rupam warned, 'or we won't be able to lift it. And no, I haven't. Practised, trained, even fought a few demons out on missions. But not here. Not like this.' He sounded nervous.

'What if they get inside?'

'They'll send us to Hell.'

Ben wasn't sure if that was a joke, an expression or the truth. He didn't ask. He didn't want to know.

'What now?'

'We get out there and help. I need matches to light the lantern.' He found some in a cupboard by the sink. 'This will be useful too,' Rupam said, taking out a bottle of surface cleaner that had a spray attachment on the top. 'Not much left – empty it out and you can fill it with water.'

'Holy water pistol,' Ben said.

They both laughed, but it was nervous laughter.

Outside the night sky was split by a sudden flash of lightning. There was no accompanying thunder.

'They're breaking through,' Rupam said.

The battle was a blur to Ben. Huge security lights illuminated the grounds of the house and the main driveway. He had taken up position with Rupam near a large tree which they both thought might offer some cover. Gemma and Knight were on the other side of the drive. Maria stood in the middle of the drive, the wind whipping at her dark hair and blowing it round her face as she held her sword aloft. For once, her sour expression exactly matched the situation.

Ben felt out of place and afraid. He was standing in the shadows holding a spray bottle of water. Even Rupam seemed better-armed. The light from his lantern was directed by the mirrors inside and focused by the lenses at the front, so that it shone out like a flickering torch beam.

But there was little time to complain. Almost as soon as they had taken up their positions, the attack began. An *invisible* attack, accompanied by a chittering, giggling sound. The air seemed to shimmer – though that might have been the tears in Ben's eyes.

Maria sliced with her sword, practised moves that were at once elegant and brutal. Ben saw the sword slow and rebound as it struck the hidden creatures. He heard the ring of silver on their stony bodies.

Gemma was reciting from the book, shouting into the increasing wind. Beside her, Knight held his phone open in one hand and aimed his handgun with the other.

Rupam leapt out from behind the tree, scanning his beam of lantern light across the grounds like a searchlight. Confused images appeared in the light as it moved – creatures made briefly visible. Shrieking in agony and steaming in the heat from the light beam.

Ben had his own phone out, copying Knight. But the image was a wash of swirling colour. He squirted the water at anything that moved, or he thought moved. And into empty space. Everywhere. On the tiny screen he saw something like an upright, grinning rat get a face full of the spray. It exploded into dust.

Then he saw a group of three spiky, snarling creatures rush at Gemma. She stood her ground, reading from the book, but Ben could see she was trembling. He ran forward, squeezing the trigger of the spray bottle. The creatures clawed at Gemma, but she kept reading. One of them fell away, clutching its angular head. Another caught a burst of spray and staggered back, snarling in pain.

A shot from Knight's gun blew the last of the creatures into fiery pieces and Gemma was safe again.

Maria gave a yell of what might have been anger or elation, and charged down the drive. The silver blade whirled and cut, sliced and stabbed.

'Behind you!' Rupam shouted. He swung the lantern and picked out a hideous creature like a gnarled, bald garden gnome standing behind Maria, its clawed hands outstretched. Smoke rose from the creature's fingers as it froze in pain and fear.

Then Maria spun round, the sword connected, and Ben looked quickly away.

A shot from Knight's gun exploded apparently in mid-air. A fireball spattered over the shape of an imp-like demon. Its wings flapped furiously as it rose out of the fire, shrieking in rage.

Rupam had run after Maria and Ben followed. Knight and Gemma hurried to join them – all five standing across the driveway, daring the invisible attackers to try again.

On his phone, Ben could see the creatures scuttling away. He didn't have to ask if they would return.

'That was the creature Ben saw,' Gemma told them, pointing. 'Daniella Lawton's Grotesque.'

'Leading the assault,' Knight agreed. 'She'll be watching from somewhere nearby.' His voice was grave. 'We were lucky. Perhaps they didn't expect such fierce resistance. They expected to sneak in and take us by surprise. But they'll soon be back and we'll have to retreat into the house. I need to make sure Mrs Bailey's finished chalking out our defences.'

'We'll be fine,' Maria told him.

Knight nodded. 'No risks,' he warned. 'Hold them off as best you can, but fall back to the house and we'll wait there for Morton's team and Growl.'

'Right, new positions,' Maria ordered as soon as Knight was gone. 'Gemma, you stay with me. Rupam, with Ben.'

'I don't need looking after,' Ben said.

'Rupam does.'

It was the closest to a joke that Ben had heard from Maria. He turned away to hide his amusement, pretending to be looking for a new hiding place to wait for the inevitable attack. And suddenly he was aware of movement in the gloom by the tree where he and Rupam had sheltered before. A figure – waving.

It was Sam.

Without waiting for Rupam, Ben ran back to the tree. The wind was thrashing the branches, making twigs and leaves fall in a swirl.

'What are you doing?' Ben had to shout to be heard, even though he was standing right next to her. 'Where have you been? I thought – by the lake – I thought I'd imagined it all.'

'I can't be seen here. Not by *them*.' Sam was looking down towards the gates, in the direction from which the first attack had come.

'But why not? How did you find me? Have you come to help?' He had so many questions he didn't know where to start. 'Why did you leave me?'

Sam was still looking down the drive. 'You need to find a way to turn this to your advantage. They know where you are now – where Knight is based. You need to find out where *they* are.'

'Great, yeah, easy. How do I do that? You just turn up after all this time and start giving orders.'

Sam was looking over Ben's shoulder. 'I'm sorry,' she said. 'It's good to see you, Ben.'

But he barely heard her as he turned to see Rupam running over to join them.

'It's all right. It's only Rupam. He'll –'

But Sam had gone, swallowed up into the night.

'You all right?' Rupam asked.

'Fine.' Ben said, still staring into the darkness. 'That was . . . Did you see anyone?'

'What, just now?' Rupam shook his head. 'You sure you're all right?'

Ben nodded quickly. Was his imagination playing tricks on him? Was he going mad? But Sam had been *here*. He wanted to tell Rupam, but instead he heard himself saying, 'I was just thinking, there must be some way to turn all this to our advantage. Some way to find out who these people are and where they've come from. That woman, whatever her name is . . .'

'Daniella Lawton,' Rupam said at once.

'Yes – she must be nearby. Gemma saw her Grotesque. Knight said they stay close together, didn't he? So maybe we can find her.'

'How does that help?'

Ben wasn't sure it did. 'We could get her car number or something,' he said, stooping to refill his spray bottle from the cooking pot full of water beside the tree. But it sounded a bit lame. 'Just – do *something* rather than wait here for those things to attack again.'

Rupam was frowning. 'You're right. If we can find her, then maybe the Grotesque will call off the attack. If it knows she's in danger . . .' He was nodding enthusiastically, excited by the idea. 'Yes, it might work.'

'We can sort her out with a squirt of water and a bit of light from your magic lantern,' Ben joked.

Suddenly it wasn't seeming such a good idea. But Rupam wasn't listening.

'Come on – before they attack again!'

He set off quickly through the grounds, keeping to the darker shadows as he led the way towards the main gates. The lenses over the lantern were set to cast just a pale glow that was enough to illuminate the ground in front of them.

'We should tell the others,' Ben said.

'And have Maria stop us?'

'Better she stops us than something else does,' Ben murmured.

From behind came the sound of a renewed

attack. The clang of Maria's sword, her shouts, the shriek of the creatures of the night.

'We have to go back,' Ben shouted above the noise.

'No! It's too late. We have to draw them off.'

Ben could tell that Rupam would not be dissuaded. But a quick glance at the screen on his mobile showed him dozens of creatures pouring through the main gates and up the driveway. If they were to create a distraction, then they needed to get to the woman some other way.

'They haven't spotted us,' Rupam said. 'They seem completely focused on getting past Maria.'

'They'll see us if we head for the gates. Over the wall,' Ben decided. 'I'll give you a bunk-up. Give us your lantern.'

He made a step out of his clasped hands and heaved Rupam up. The wall was high, but Ben could just reach up enough to pass Rupam back the lantern. With the light balanced on the top, next to Ben's spray bottle, Rupam reached back down to haul Ben up to join him.

On the other side of the wall, they could see the woman standing by her car, just outside the grounds, the headlights shining past her so she seemed to be emitting the light from her dark silhouette.

Rupam aimed the lantern, moving different lenses in and out of position. But it had no effect.

'She's no demon,' he grumbled. 'She's real enough.'

'Come on,' Ben said.

He leapt down from the wall. It was a long way and his legs jarred with the impact even though he bent his knees and fell forward.

Rupam dropped down beside him. 'What now?'

'Punch her? I don't know. But we need her to call off those things.'

There was another noise now. Coming from the sky – a steady thump of sound. A bright light bit through the night and a dark shape appeared over the distant trees on the far side of the estate, growing rapidly louder and larger.

'She's getting some serious help!' Ben yelled in Rupam's ear. 'We're done for!'

16

RUPAM WAS GRINNING. 'THAT'S CAPTAIN Morton. Got to be. We'll be all right now.'

'Not if she just gets away,' Ben said, watching the shape of the helicopter grow more distinct as it got closer.

It was coming in to land in front of the house. The searchlight picked out the figure of Maria – sword raised over and behind her head, ready to strike down at the attacking ghouls.

The woman had pushed herself away from the car and run to the gates to see what was happening. Even over the sound of the helicopter and the wind, Ben could hear her cursing.

'Now! Quick,' he hissed to Rupam, and ran.

He reached the car and pulled open the back door. He ducked inside.

'What are you doing?' Rupam dragged Ben out again. 'Don't be crazy!'

'She's coming back,' Ben said. 'Hurry up.'

He pushed the door shut, trying not to make too much noise. They were the opposite side of the car from the woman, so he hoped she hadn't seen them as they crouched down and hurried away.

'We need to get back,' Rupam said. 'If Knight finds out what we've been up to he'll go mad.'

'We were helping,' Ben insisted.

'It was a stupid idea. We should have stayed and waited with Maria and Gemma like he said.'

Ben didn't waste time arguing. Rupam didn't realise he'd already done what he set out to do. He helped Rupam back up on to the wall. They collected the lantern and spray bottle before dropping down again on the other side.

Morton's men had gone straight into action. Half a dozen dark figures in combat uniforms were making their way along the drive towards the gates. One of them turned and fired. Ben caught the briefest glimpse of a creature like a two-legged lizard as it flared into view for a moment. Then it exploded – just as if Ben had sprayed it.

'Neat,' Rupam whispered to Ben. 'They're firing capsules of holy water. Morton's people have been trying to get that to work for ages. The glass usually breaks in the barrel when you fire.'

A creature exploded nearby.

The soldiers continued to work their way down the drive. But it was slow progress. Ben could see now that they were wearing goggles, like infrared night-sights. He guessed they worked the same way as the phones, showing up the demons and their aura. He reached for his own phone, forgetting for a moment that he no longer had it . . .

Another figure was walking rapidly down the drive, flanked by the soldiers. He wore a long dark cloak and he had his arms open as if delivering a blessing – or a curse.

The Reverend Alistair Growl's lips were constantly moving as he spoke: prayers, spells, words of power – whatever they were it was effective. His face was twisted into a rictus of anger and determination. He was like another person from the kindly, talkative clergyman that Ben had first met at the graveyard. Ahead of Growl the air exploded. A sequence of coloured blasts as he approached.

The wind was dying down. Ben couldn't see the creatures. But he could hear them as they hurried back down the drive. And in the distance he thought he heard shouts and screams, then the sound of a car starting up and pulling away . . .

Knight was waiting for them outside the house, Maria standing silently beside him. Mrs Bailey stood in the doorway. Knight glared at Ben before turning his anger on Rupam as they approached.

'What on earth do you think you were doing, abandoning Gemma and Maria?'

Rupam hung his head. 'I'm sorry, sir. We just thought that we ought to do something. That we ought to try to turn this situation to our advantage.'

Hearing his own words – or rather Sam's – played back to him, Ben decided he ought to confess. 'It was my idea. I'm sorry.'

'You're new to all this,' Knight said, without looking away from Rupam. 'You have a lot to learn. I had hoped that Rupam had already learned it.'

'But there's no problem,' Rupam protested.

Even as he said it, Ben could tell Rupam was wrong. He looked from Knight to Maria to Mrs Bailey, feeling suddenly cold inside as a question formed in his mind. Maria answered it before he spoke.

'They got Gemma,' she said. 'You weren't here,' she added bitterly, 'and they got Gemma. I couldn't stop them all. They grabbed her and took her away.'

'What?' Rupam sounded shocked.

Ben swallowed, his throat dry. He was more afraid to speak up again than he had been during the attack. 'We might know where they're taking her, where the woman is going.'

'That's right,' Rupam said. 'We saw her car. I can remember the number.'

'You think Morton's people will be able to track it?' Knight asked. His tone suggested that it wasn't likely.

'I think Webby will,' Ben said. 'You told me that he can trace my mobile phone. That he can tell exactly where it is at any time.'

Knight turned to look at Ben for the first time. 'Don't you know where your phone is? Have you lost that as well as Gemma?' He sounded about ready to explode.

Ben shook his head. 'I haven't lost it. Not really. I know exactly where it is.'

'So where is it?'

'It's hidden under the passenger seat in Daniella's Lawton's car.'

Knight's demeanour changed almost immediately. Suddenly he was all action again, hurrying to talk to Webby, who was still closeted in his cellar office.

Mrs Bailey offered coffee and sandwiches to Captain Morton and his men, but the soldiers headed straight off to other duties. Growl was still standing by the open gates to the drive – Daniella Lawton or one of her minions had cut through the chain that held them shut. Ben and the other children went back to the playroom, tired and downcast by events.

'You were good with that sword,' Ben said to Maria as she slumped down on the sofa, her usual scowl back in place.

'I was useless,' she told him. 'I could hardly see what I was doing. I couldn't even protect Gemma.' She turned away. 'Why did they come for Gemma? Why now? Something's changed. Something's going on.'

'It is indeed.' Knight was standing in the doorway, looking solemn. 'It's time I told you all what's happening. At least, what might be happening. So far it's been just rumours and guesswork. But after tonight . . .' He looked round at them all. 'Lecture hall in ten minutes please.'

His expression softened. 'Ben, would you come to my study for a few minutes first please? There's something I need to tell you. Something I should have told you when we first met.'

Ben looked at the others, wondering why he'd been singled out. Rupam looked away. Maria didn't meet his eyes.

'Is it about what happened to Sam?' Ben asked. But Knight had gone.

Knight was standing in front of his desk, leaning back on it. He gestured for Ben to sit down.

'Carstairs Endeavour,' he said. 'I'm sure you're right and he was the man you saw at the home. Only Endeavour would dare attack us here. He wanted to strike quickly, before we were prepared. He had the Lawton woman watching that school, so maybe the whole thing was a set-up to bring us there so she could follow. There are very few people who know about this place.' He smiled thinly. 'It's one of the reasons why I was so impressed that you found us.'

'So who is this Endeavour exactly?'

'A man who played with fire a long time ago. He dropped out of sight for a while, but recently he's been active again. When I first encountered him, he was trying to learn the secrets of Gabriel Diablo, to track down the artefacts taken by the Memento Mori all those years ago . . .'

Ben shook his head. 'Sorry . . .' He hadn't a clue what the man was talking about.

'Doesn't matter. I'll explain it all to everyone in the lecture hall in a few minutes. All you need to know for now is that Carstairs Endeavour is a deranged and ambitious man. He's rich and he's powerful, but he wants to be even more rich, and he'll settle for nothing less than total power. Oh, I don't mean he wants to rule the world. But he wants to be able to influence the people who do.'

'How can he do that? And what's it got to do with us? With me?' He wanted to add, 'With Sam?' but he didn't.

'The Grotesques, and other powers that Endeavour and his followers must have, are trivial. Of course, they're dangerous enough, but on the grand scale they're minor league. About ten years ago –' Knight paused, his eyebrows tightening together as he stared off into space – 'a bit more than that now. Doesn't matter. But Carstairs Endeavour tried to summon a powerful demon called Mortagula – summon it and bind it to his will.'

Ben leaned forward. 'Did he do it?'

'Almost. And now I think he feels powerful enough to try again. He lacked knowledge and he lacked certain artefacts. As a result, the summoning failed. But even so there was a terrible cost. A life.'

Ben felt cold. He had so many questions he wanted to ask, but none of them would come into focus in his mind. He couldn't think of the words to frame them. What did this have to do with Sam? Or Gemma?

'To bring a demon like that out of Hell, you need to offer something in return. A soul, a life, call it what you will. The more innocent and uncorrupted the better. The more potential that life has which will be left unfulfilled, the more power it commands.'

'You mean, like a *sacrifice*?' Ben said. His voice was husky and dry.

Knight nodded. He wiped his eyes with the back of his hand. 'Children, powerful children with the Sight, have gone missing before. They've been taken, I believe, by Endeavour. And now he's got Gemma.'

Ben could see what Knight was thinking. But he was wrong – he had to be. 'Sam?'

'Your sister was very powerful – the most gifted child I've come across. She was taken by Endeavour. She was exactly what he needed. And he took her.'

'Sam's in danger, then.' Ben stood up. 'We have to find her. Warn her – *help* her.'

But Knight was shaking his head. 'It was so long ago, Ben. I'm sorry.'

'But it isn't too late. It can't be.'

Ben almost laughed out loud with relief as he saw that Sam had stepped into the room. She was standing by the door, watching them. Knight hadn't noticed her yet, but if he turned, just slightly, he couldn't miss her.

'Sam!'

Knight put his hand on Ben's shoulder. 'I know,' he said quietly, 'I know. It's a shock. I'm sorry. I should have told you before that she might . . .'

Sam walked slowly across to join them. She stood beside Knight, looking down at Ben.

'Sorry,' she mouthed.

'What do you mean?' Ben looked from one to the other, confused. 'Sam?'

'I told you nothing would keep us apart, Ben,' Sam said. 'I'll always be here for you. Always.'

Knight didn't look at her. He didn't seem to hear her, or even know she was there. 'The fact he now needs Gemma, that he took such a risk to get her, can mean only one thing, I'm afraid.' The man's eyes were filled with tears. 'Your sister is dead, Ben.'

Ben could see that Sam was crying too. Tears ran down her face just as he could feel them running down his own. She blinked – as he did – then wiped at her cheeks.

'I'm sorry, Ben. So sorry,' Sam said.

Ben looked at Knight. 'But can't you *see* –' he began.

'Look, Ben, we can talk more later. Our priority now has to be to save Gemma. But I just couldn't keep it from you any longer.'

'But, Sam – she's . . .'

Ben's voice became a sob as he realised there were just the two of them. Ben and Knight. Alone in an empty room.

17

'SO WHAT'S IT LIKE, THEN – BEING DEAD?' BEN murmured to Sam as she sat next to him in the lecture hall.

On the other side of Ben, Rupam glanced at him as if wondering why he was talking to himself.

'Damned if I know,' Sam said. No one paid any attention to her except Ben. 'That's a joke,' she added when he didn't reply. 'Just pretend I'm not here.'

'Another joke?'

'Are you all right?' Rupam asked. He put his hand over Ben's, which was resting on the desk in front of them. 'Mrs Bailey told us what Knight said about your sister. I'm really sorry she's . . . gone.'

'She promised,' Ben said quietly. 'Sam always keeps her promises.'

Maria sat down in the empty seat the other side of Ben – the seat where moments before Sam had been sitting. She looked at Ben sadly, her eyes moist.

'We've all lost someone,' she said.

He couldn't reply. He stared down at the polished wooden desk and he could see every detail of the grain, every aspect of every knothole. Until the image blurred and he had to blink away his tears again.

Knight's voice jolted Ben back to reality. He realised that Growl and Captain Morton were sitting further along in the same row as himself, Rupam and Maria. Mrs Bailey was a couple of rows behind.

'To begin with, thanks to you all for your efforts tonight. We've faced a formidable threat and we have suffered a terrible loss. The threat is only just beginning. I'll tell you exactly what we're up against in a moment, so far as I know anyway. But first, well done to Ben for giving us a good lead on Endeavour and his cohorts. Once we know where they have taken Gemma, then there's a chance – a good chance – we can save her.'

Knight smiled at Ben, who struggled to manage a smile back.

'Webby is tracking Ben's phone,' Knight went on. 'He'll let us know as soon as it seems to have arrived at its destination.'

Rupam waved his hand to ask a question. 'Can't

we track Daniella Lawton by satellite, like we tracked her here?'

It was Captain Morton who answered. 'I managed to borrow a US spy satellite for that. Wasn't easy and we've lost the window of opportunity now, I'm afraid. We were lucky to get a look-in the first time. There just happened to be a satellite we could use in the right place at the right time.'

'Webby can give us the exact location from the phone's global positioning system,' Knight said. 'Assuming Miss Lawton goes to report to Endeavour, we'll know where he is.'

'Unless she changes car on the way,' Maria said.

'Trust misery-guts to cheer us all up,' Rupam muttered, making Ben smile for the first time since he had spoken to Knight.

'What do we do when we find Endeavour?' Growl asked. 'Do we know what he's up to?'

Knight nodded thoughtfully. 'Carstairs Endeavour is an ambitious man. He has considerable power and money, and he craves more of both. We know he already has the knowledge and ability to capture and bind Grotesques and lesser demons like those that attacked us here. We know that he is not working alone. I have a good idea what he intends, but much of it must of necessity be supposition and extrapolation.'

'What's that mean?' Ben whispered to Rupam.

'It means he's guessing,' Rupam whispered back.

'It's more than just guesswork,' Knight said.

Rupam muttered an apology and Ben felt himself blushing that they'd been overheard.

'Sorry,' Ben said.

'For some time, we've been getting reports of increased activity, more sightings and summonings. More manifestations for no apparent reason, like the Grave Lady we saw the other day. I now believe that something is stirring in the void between this world and the realm that we call Hell.'

'It's like a storm,' Growl announced. 'Activity in the void stirs up everything, heightens it, makes it worse. You are right about that woman in the graveyard – a very ordinary apparition suddenly manifesting more often and more agitated. I can feel it myself.' He thumped his fist into his chest. 'In here, I feel it.'

'A demon storm,' Ben said.

'Could be,' Knight admitted.

'But what is causing it?' Mrs Bailey asked.

'So far,' Knight said, 'Endeavour and his followers have been relatively low-key. Using knowledge

I suspect they acquired from old records of the Memento Mori and techniques gleaned from the writings of Gabriel Diablo, they have summoned forth demons.'

'What's he talking about?' Ben whispered.

But Rupam waved him to silence, concentrating as Knight continued speaking.

'Small, fairly weak demons, and creatures like the Grotesques. These Diabolists led by Endeavour are probably powerful and influential people, like Daniella Lawton. They call upon the power of the demons to help them. But, as I say, that power is limited.'

'How do they use their power?' Morton asked.

'In this case, I can only guess. Perhaps an opponent taken ill at a crucial point in a business meeting. The certainty that someone is lying. Crucial financial data mysteriously wiped from every computer and backup of another company . . . Even trivial hauntings so that builders are scared off a vital development site . . . You can imagine the *edge* that a Grotesque would give them.'

'And now they're trading up to bigger demons?' Maria said. 'Is that what you're telling us?'

'It is. Endeavour and his colleagues want more. So far they're just playing. Think of the wealth and power they could achieve if they had all of Gabriel Diablo's fabled ability . . . And that is what they are after.'

Ben put his hand up. 'Can I ask a question?'

'Of course.'

'Who is this Gabriel Diablo you keep going on about? What did he do? What's Endeavour hoping to get?' He was aware that everyone was looking at him. 'Sorry,' he said. 'Maybe I missed that lesson.'

'Gabriel Diablo,' Growl said, 'was the most accomplished alchemist and mystic of the seventeenth century. He tried to summon forth a tremendously powerful creature from beyond this world. A demon, if you like. The demon to destroy all other demons – Mortagula. And Diablo almost succeeded.'

'That is what Endeavour is after,' Knight said. 'If he has found the fabled artefacts that Diablo used in his summoning, he can recreate Diablo's ceremony. And with Gemma as well, he can call forth Mortagula.'

'And what will that give him?' Ben asked.

'The power to control the world,' Knight said. 'Or to destroy it.' He looked round at his audience. 'We ought to remind ourselves of what Diablo was trying to achieve. Let me tell you what happened all those years ago . . .'

The preparations were complete. Everything was in its appointed place. The chamber was accurate to the last fraction of an inch. The candles were exactly spaced around the circle within which Gabriel Diablo stood, prepared. And the child was dead, her congealing blood staining the floor beneath his feet.

Diablo made one final check. The Dagger was on the altar stone at one point of the red pentacle painted on the floor. The two Volumes of Power were at the points of the pentacle either side of the altar. The Amulet and the Crystal were positioned on the final two points.

The circular chamber itself mirrored the pentacle. The vaulted ceiling dipped at the points of the star within the circle. The edges of the underground room were lost in shadow.

The only sound was the steady click of a brass clock as it ticked away the seconds to midnight.

The Time of Summoning.

The chimes echoed round the stone-walled room. Diablo drew the hood of his blood-red cloak up over his head. He opened the First Volume, *The Book of Darkness Rising*, careful not to let its covers fall outside the painted lines. Like the Second Volume, *The Book of Lost Souls,* it was bound in leather, braced with bands of Hellstorm forged by Diablo himself.

Finally, Diablo was ready to speak the words of power. The Summoning. The Latin text blurred in front of him and he blinked until the text was clear again. Handwritten, ornate, beautifully formed words. He didn't need to see them, as he knew them well already. But he could not afford to make any mistakes tonight. He took a deep breath and intoned the first word — the name of the creature he was about to summon forth from the depths of Hell itself: 'Mortagula.'

The word echoed round the chamber, hanging in the air like the incense from the burners positioned outside the pentacle. Their thick vapour added to the smoke from the candles along the rim of the circle. The flames guttered at the sound of the demon's name — as if caught in an impossible breeze.

Diablo spoke the first of the incantations. The air, already heavy with smoke, seemed to thicken in front of him. Above the low altar stone a shape was forming out of the cloudy vapours. A massive, sinister face. Its features were ragged and torn, the horns on its head stunted and broken.

But as Diablo moved to the next incantation, the figure began to fill out. It became gradually more solid, the horns growing, curling, extending . . .

The words of the third incantation were punctuated by a steady thump. It might have been the click of the clock or the beating of Diablo's own excited heart. Or the sound of booted feet hurrying down the steps outside the chamber.

The fourth incantation. The smoke-filled apparition was almost solid. Massive claws raked through the air. Cloven hooves scraped across the top of the altar and Diablo snatched up the Dagger. Its Hellstorm blade glinted in the trembling candlelight as he held it aloft — the symbol of his power over Mortagula.

The creature snarled in rage, the claws pulling back as it realised what it was facing. Beneath the scarlet hood of his cloak, Diablo's features twisted into a satisfied smile.

But his smile froze as the creature in front of him started to laugh. Smoke snorted from its flaring nostrils and it raised a huge arm, clawed finger extended, pointing past Diablo to the back of the chamber.

Where the door smashed open.

The candles nearest the door were snuffed out. Thin trails of black smoke coiled up from the dead wicks. Mortagula's laughter echoed round the chamber, louder even than the stamp of the figures rushing in.

They wore the armour and carried the swords of Crusader Knights. On their tabards was emblazoned the symbol of the cross held in a clenched fist — soldiers of the Memento Mori.

They could not enter the circle. They dared not. Diablo stared at them defiantly. Just one more incantation. Just one more and Mortagula would be completely formed, bound entirely to his will. Even the Memento Mori — the secret soldiers of the Pope — couldn't stop him then.

Another figure stepped into the chamber. Hooded and cloaked like Diablo, he pushed through the circle of knights and stood facing the altar. He threw back his black hood and spread his arms as he started to speak.

Diablo stared in horror. He recognised the words, the secret opening spell that would allow the knights to cross the circle and enter the pentacle. Stammering, he hurried to complete the final incantation. But his voice faltered as he stared at the face of the chanting figure before him.

It was a face drained of all colour and flesh. Sunken, parchment-like brittle skin was stretched over a skull. A spider's web of pale blue veins throbbed across the completely bald head. The Grand Master of the Memento Mori smiled, and despite all the terrible things he had seen in his life, Diablo thought this was the most frightening.

He dropped the Dagger.

It clattered to the stone floor of the chamber, out of the circle — out of reach.

Before Diablo could even begin to think what to do, an ice-cold hand closed on his throat.

He twisted round, expecting to see one of the knights of the Memento Mori stepping into the circle to grab him, sword raised ready to strike.

Instead, he stared into the face of Hell. Mortagula's laughter filled his ears. The demonic creature's hideous features filled his vision. Its cold, smoky claws bit into his neck. The massive creature stepped off the altar, backing away into the darkness of the chamber, dragging Diablo with it, into the smoke. Back to Hell . . .

There was silence for several moments after they had gone.

'The beast, My Lord?' one of the knights asked, his voice trembling. 'Is it banished?'

'And Diablo with it,' the Grand Master said. He turned to survey the chamber. 'Collect up the artefacts. We need to study Diablo's hellish work, so we can prevent others from following the same misguided path.'

'My Lord.'

The knights moved quickly to obey, each of them wanting to spend as little time as possible in the chamber. One knight closed and picked up *The Book of Darkness Rising*, another took *The Book of Lost Souls*. The Grand Master lifted the Crystal from its place at the edge of the pentacle. A knight handed him the Amulet.

The Grand Master took one last look round the room. Most of the candles had gone out.

'Our work here is done. I think we can leave this cold, damp island and return to Rome.' He nodded with satisfaction. 'Seal the chamber behind us.'

'And the house above?'

'Burn it.'

The knights filed out of the chamber. Last to leave was the Grand Master himself. He hesitated for a second in the doorway, but did not look back.

If he had, then perhaps he might have caught the glint of Hellstorm metal in the dying light of the last of the candles. Perhaps he might have seen the Dagger lying by the wall of the chamber. The Dagger with which Diablo had hoped to bind the most powerful of all demons to his will . . .

'We cannot rely on the Memento Mori to stop Endeavour as they stopped Diablo,' Knight said.

'Why not?' Ben asked.

'In 1729 the Pope dissolved the Memento Mori,' Growl said. 'They'd outlived the Inquisition, but become arrogant and uncontrollable. Without papal "sponsorship", the organisation was forced to work secretly. But over time . . .'

'To all intents and purposes, they no longer exist,' Knight said.

'The artefacts they took from Diablo's ceremony were scattered and lost, and the members of the group went into hiding,' Growl said.

'So does Endeavour have these artefacts?' Maria asked.

'Unlikely,' Knight said. 'He has some understanding, some idea of how to perform the Summoning. And a little knowledge is a dangerous thing. If he has Mortagula at his beck and call, that's bad enough. But a creature of that power loose in the world with nothing to restrain it . . .' He shook his head.

'Then we have to stop Endeavour,' Ben said. 'Right?'

'Right,' Rupam agreed.

'But we have to find him first,' Maria pointed out. 'And we have to rescue Gemma. The longer we sit around here talking about it . . .'

Her voice choked off and she looked down. It was the most emotional Ben had ever seen her.

There was a warbling sound from the other side of the lecture hall. Someone's mobile.

'Sorry,' Mrs Bailey said, already checking her phone. 'Text message from Webby. He says that Ben's mobile has been stationary for a while now. The phone's detecting a huge amount of paranormal activity in the immediate area. He's triangulated the co-ordinates and it's a house in an isolated village in Cornwall.'

'Just the sort of place to summon forth a great demon,' Captain Morton said.

'Indeed,' Knight replied. 'Mrs Bailey, I need you here to organise things. See if you can contact Madam Sosostram, will you, please? Morton, re-equip your team and get them back from Hereford as fast as you can. Meet them on the way and tell them what's going on. Maria, come with me.'

'Where are we going?' Maria asked.

'A house in an isolated village in Cornwall.' Knight checked his watch. 'It's gone nine o'clock and we have to get there before midnight. Before Endeavour summons Mortagula again.'

18

KNIGHT WAS FORCED TO LET RUPAM AND BEN come along as well – he didn't have the time or the energy to argue with them. As everyone assembled in the hallway, ready to leave, Mrs Bailey came out of her office.

'Madam Sosostram will join you there,' she reported. 'Apparently she has to feed the cats first.' She raised her eyebrows. 'You know what she's like. Sure you won't be requiring me?'

Knight shook his head. 'No time for the subtle approach. You're more use to us here, if that's OK?' He checked his watch, then clapped his hands together. 'Right, come on, everyone. No time to lose.'

Maria went with Knight, while Ben and Rupam travelled with Growl. The Reverend had an ancient car that shook so much as it moved that Ben was afraid it would fall apart. There seemed to be no suspension in the back seats, where he was sitting. Rupam had insisted on taking the passenger seat, claiming he sometimes got carsick. Ben guessed that he'd travelled with Growl before.

But Ben wasn't alone in the back of the car.

'Why did you lie to me?' he asked Sam.

The combined sound of the engine and the exhaust meant that Growl and Rupam couldn't hear him.

'I didn't lie,' Sam protested. 'I just didn't remember what happened to me after I was taken from the home. I still don't.'

'You might have told me you were a *ghost*.'

'Is that what I am?' She smiled. 'You sure?'

'I'm serious,' Ben told her.

'I know.'

'Why can't you take this seriously?'

'I am the one who's dead. That's pretty serious.'

Ben looked out of the window. All he could see was his own reflection staring back at him. 'The way things are going, I might join you,' he muttered. 'Gemma too.'

At once he regretted his anger. It wasn't Sam's fault. None of this was Sam's fault.

'Look, I'm sorry,' Ben said, turning back. But he was alone in the back of the car.

Rupam had turned round in his seat and was leaning towards Ben. 'Sorry about what?'

'Oh, I don't know. Everything. I just don't feel like I'm helping much.' He had to shout for Rupam to hear clearly.

'Hey, it's because of you that we know where to find Endeavour.'

'I know. But that also means that whatever happens when we get there – it's my fault.'

It was after eleven when they arrived. Growl parked next to Knight's car, which was already there.

The street was a very ordinary one in a small village. The houses were of different ages and designs, all set back from the road. Ben recognised Daniella Lawton's car parked on the drive of a large detached house. The house was square, with steps up to a central front door that had windows either side. Upstairs windows balanced the ones below, giving the building a symmetry like a child's drawing of an idealised house. There were lights on behind the curtains and a security light illuminated the front driveway.

A man was standing outside the house, stamping his feet in the cold. As he turned and walked slowly across the front of the house, his jacket flapped open – revealing a plain white shirt and a dark shoulder holster strapped in position.

Knight was standing in the shadows on the other side of the street, with Maria and Madam Sosostram.

'It's most definitely the right place,' Growl told them all. 'I can feel it in here.' He tapped his chest, then his forehead. 'Here too, come to that.'

'Plus there's an armed guard,' Rupam pointed out.

'Which is a bit of a clue,' Madam Sosostram added. 'At least he doesn't have a Grotesque.'

'Probably just a hired thug.' Maria said. 'So what do we do? We can't just walk in.'

'And we can't wait for Captain Morton,' Knight added. 'Gemma is in the most terrible danger and we're cutting it fine as it is. We have no idea what we shall find inside.'

'Then I suggest we charm our way in and rescue that poor little girl,' Madam Sosostram said. 'Let me have a word with that nice young man and see what I can do.'

Ben watched in amazement as Madam Sosostram handed Knight her walking stick, then shambled across the road towards the house.

'What's she doing?' he said. 'That guard won't be worried by a little old lady.'

Growl smiled. 'Watch and learn,' he replied. 'Though I'm afraid we're a little too far away to get the full benefit.'

The guard outside the house also seemed surprised as Madam Sosostram approached him. His hand strayed inside his jacket, but as she spoke to him he seemed to relax. The old lady put her hand out and stroked it down his cheek. It was a strange gesture, Ben thought – out of character, and more likely to make the man suspicious than win his confidence.

But the man pressed his own hand against Madam Sosostram's. Ben caught a hint of her croaky laughter. The man was smiling as Madam Sosostram stepped away from him. She walked across the driveway, towards the side of the house. Then she paused and looked back at the man for a long moment, before continuing on her way.

To Ben's astonishment, the man hurried after her. 'How'd she do that?' he asked.

Rupam grinned. 'You'll work it out one day. Maybe.'

'Come on,' Knight urged, leading them quickly and quietly across the road.

Madam Sosostram was coming back and there was no sign of the guard. She pointed to empty space just in front of Ben as she approached. 'Sorry about that one. It was guarding the back door.'

Growl stepped forward. His face twisted into a sudden fury and he pointed a crooked finger across the drive, towards where Ben was standing, speaking rapidly and quietly.

Ben heard a confused mixture of a snarl and a popping sound. There was a brief flash of light right in front of his face where Madam Sosostram had pointed, and Growl lowered his arm.

'Cool,' Rupam said in a hushed voice, running up to Ben. 'The way you just stood there and faced down the Lawton woman's Grotesque.'

'Like it wasn't even there,' Maria added. 'And it was jumping up right at you.'

Ben swallowed. He had known nothing about it until Growl destroyed the creature. Without his phone, he realised, he couldn't even see what they were fighting. And everyone else assumed he had some of the same power and ability to see the demons that they did.

There was no time to put them right, even if he wanted to. Knight was at the front door now.

Madam Sosostram hurried over and handed him a key she must have got from the guard.

'Ready?' Knight asked quietly. 'Growl, you take Ben and Rupam and see if you can find a way in round the back. Ladies – with me, here.'

'He's just trying to keep us out of the way,' Rupam grumbled.

Ben wasn't about to complain. He didn't know exactly how extraordinary the events of this evening were for Rupam and the others, but he was still trying to understand what was happening – to him, to Sam, to all of them . . . An extra few minutes when he wasn't being attacked by invisible demons could only be a bonus.

There was a narrow alleyway between the side of the house and the garden fence. Growl led the way, stepping over the body of the unconscious guard. Ben wondered what Madam Sosostram could have hit him with. A spell, maybe.

At the back of the house was a long garden, mostly laid to lawn but with tall trees either side and a hedge at the end. Like the front, the whole area was lit by a security light mounted high on the wall of the house.

'I'd have thought he'd choose somewhere isolated, not in a village,' Ben said.

'The location of a Summoning is very important,' Growl said. 'This house may lie on ancient ley lines or at the meeting point of magnetic influences.'

'Or it might be handy for the supermarket,' Rupam added.

'That too.' Growl smiled. Then he seemed to sway on his feet as if dizzy, grabbing Rupam's shoulder for support.

'Are you all right?' Ben asked.

Rupam shot him a look that said, 'Be quiet!'

Growl had regained his balance now and turned to glare at Ben. His eyes were narrowed and dark. His face was once more set in a grim, determined expression.

'Don't ask stupid questions,' he snarled. 'We don't have time for such childishness. There are demons and familiars all around us here, watching and waiting for the moment to strike.'

The clergyman whirled round, stabbing his finger at the empty air. There was a sound like a gust of wind. Ben felt something pass him at great speed, as if he was standing at the edge of the platform while an express train rushed by. But there was nothing there.

From inside the house came the sound of shouting. A scream – was it Gemma? Or Maria? A gunshot.

'Come on!' Growl said, making for the back door of the house.

His cape billowed out after him as he ran, with Ben and Rupam close behind.

The door was panelled with small panes of glass. Growl tried the handle, but the door was locked. He gave a grunt of annoyance, rammed his elbow through one of the glass panes and reached inside to unlock the door.

It led into a kitchen – in darkness except for a single candle standing on a worktop near the oven. Wax had melted and run down the sides of the candle, creating a bizarre, corrugated mass.

Growl ran through the kitchen and into the dark corridor beyond. Rupam was close behind him, with Ben following. Because he was last, he saw the others trip and stagger, and managed to stop before he too fell over the shapes on the floor of the corridor outside the kitchen.

The bodies.

Knight and Madam Sosostram.

'More visitors. We are honoured tonight.'

Ben recognised the tall, thin man who stepped from the shadows. Growl was pale with anger as he raised his hand to point at Endeavour.

But then another figure stepped out of a

doorway behind him. Daniella Lawton swung the butt of her pistol hard into Growl's head and he slumped to the floor beside Knight.

'You've killed them!' Rupam yelled, rushing forward.

'Oh, don't be so stupid,' Daniella Lawton told him. Then she turned the gun so that it was pointing at Rupam. 'Though I *ought* to kill them for what they did to my Grotesque just now.'

Ben shrank back into the shadows. Had she seen him? His eyes were now beginning to adjust to the faint, flickering light. Further down the corridor he could see more figures. Maria was there, being held tight by two men. Though she was struggling to pull free, she was having no success. He stepped back into the kitchen, keeping to the darkest shadows – out of the light of the sputtering candle.

'I think we shall have to open up a couple of the guest rooms,' Endeavour said. 'Put the children in one, the adults in the other.'

'You can't –' Maria protested, still straining to pull free of her captors.

'If she gives you any trouble, kill her,' Endeavour said, without looking at Maria. 'Is the little girl down in the cellar? We're almost ready for her.'

'You leave Gemma alone!' Maria snapped.

Endeavour ignored her. He turned and kicked at Knight's inert body with the toe of his shoe. 'It was kind of you to find her for me. The last part of the puzzle. A child of such power and vision is the very thing I need, and naive Dirk Knight had her all ready for me to collect. How very thoughtful.'

'What about the soldiers?' Daniella Lawton asked.

'No sign of them yet,' one of the men holding Maria said.

'Probably on their way,' Endeavour decided. He turned slightly to look at his stooped shoulder. 'Can I trust you to keep watch? Will you do better than your little friend, I wonder?'

Ben could hear the faint sound of high-pitched giggling, as Endeavour raised his shoulder and the weight lifted from it. He stooped down, talking to the empty air in front of him: 'If they do grace us with their presence, you'll have to hold them off. Just until midnight. After that we can make other arrangements. Now go.'

Ben shrank further back. He hoped the Grotesque wasn't coming his way. At any moment some demon or imp might spot him. He had to do something soon – but what?

'We had better make a start,' Daniella Lawton was telling Endeavour.

From his hiding place in the kitchen, Ben watched as one of the two men led Maria and Rupam away. The second hoisted Madam Sosostram on to his shoulder and followed. Ben could hear their footsteps on the stairs above him. Daniella Lawton followed Endeavour through a door. He heard their footsteps echoing on stone, descending into the cellar – where Gemma was being held captive.

Ben was desperate to run after them and try to help. But he forced himself to stay hidden in the shadows until Endeavour and Miss Lawton's footsteps had died away. Then he ran to Knight and Growl.

'Wake up,' he hissed, shaking Knight. 'Help me. What do I do?'

But they were both deeply unconscious. And now Ben could hear the footsteps coming back. The doorway that Endeavour and Daniella Lawton had gone through was filled with flickering light, so that Ben could see the stone steps leading down.

A shadow appeared in the doorway.

Another figure was at the other end of the corridor.

Ben was trapped between them.

He sprinted back towards the kitchen, hoping that no one would see him. Though he thought they must hear his heart racing if not his feet. He knew he didn't have time to get through the door and hide.

Daniella Lawton emerged from the cellar doorway. She looked towards the kitchen, where Ben was pressed to the wall by the door. If he moved, she would see him in the corridor, silhouetted against the candlelight. She took a step towards him.

'The kids are locked up safe and sound,' the man at the other end of the corridor said. 'And the old lady.'

Daniella Lawton turned. 'Good. Get these two out of here. Mortagula will deal with them very soon.'

At that moment a blast of stale air seemed to rush through the whole house. The candle in the kitchen was snuffed out. The light from the cellar danced and guttered.

The two men were dragging the bodies of Knight and Growl down the corridor. Their movements strobed in the flickering light, jerky and disjointed like an old movie.

Daniella Lawton, standing framed in the cellar doorway, gasped, 'Mortagula!'

The sound of the wind was growing. Daniella Lawton's dark hair was blowing round her face as she turned back to the cellar. Light blasted around her from below.

Ben angled his watch to catch the dazzling light. It was ten minutes to midnight. Ten minutes until Endeavour's summoning ceremony reached its climax. And Ben was the only person who could stop the arrival of the demon.

19

THE WHOLE HOUSE WAS SHAKING. DANIELLA Lawton turned slowly, trance-like, and descended the cellar steps. Ben was desperate to know what was happening down there – what was happening to Gemma.

'Find the others first,' Sam whispered, startling Ben.

'I was going to,' he hissed back at her, recovering from the surprise of her sudden arrival.

'I know.' She grabbed him in a sudden hug. 'It'll be all right. You can do it. I know you can.'

Ben held his sister's hand tightly as they made their way cautiously along the corridor. The wind from the cellar blew Sam's hair in her face. It was chill and rank.

'Upstairs,' Sam said quietly. 'They'll have locked Knight and the others in the bedrooms.'

'How do you know?'

'I'm guessing. He said "guest rooms", didn't he? But I think I've been here before. We need to be quick before the men come back down.'

There was a noise like thunder from deep below the house. A picture juddered on the wall and something fell in the kitchen, smashing on the tiled floor. There was a candle stuck with its own wax to the bottom of the banisters. Another flickered at the top. Between them was darkness. Ben took a deep breath and ran up the stairs, with Sam close behind him.

When he reached the top, she had gone. But he didn't waste time looking for her. He knew she'd be back.

There was a landing at the top of the stairs and a corridor leading off past closed doors. Candles stood at intervals along the corridor, sticking up from the wooden floorboards, flames dancing in the breeze from below.

'What have these people got against electric lighting?' Ben muttered.

He could hear the men in one of the rooms and ducked into the shadows of a doorway as they emerged, closing the door behind them. The door was heavy and the way it clanged shut told Ben it was made of metal. One of the men slid two large bolts into place, one at the top and the other at the bottom.

'They won't get out of there in a hurry,' he said.

'Even if they wake up,' the other replied.

They both laughed as they made their way down the stairs.

Ben waited until he heard them reach the bottom of the staircase, then ran to the door. The bolts were stiff, but he managed to slide them open. He hesitated, wondering if the men would come back, then opened the door. He had to push hard on it, it was so heavy.

Inside, he risked turning on the light – to see Knight, Growl and Madam Sosostram lying on the bare wooden floor. No help there. He left the door ajar. If and when they woke, hopefully they'd see the door was open. And hopefully the men wouldn't come back and discover what he'd done.

Finding Rupam and Maria was easy. Ben was prepared to look for another metal door, but he didn't have to. Even above the sounds from the cellar, he could hear them hammering to be let out.

'Thanks, Ben,' Rupam gasped as he flung open the door.

Maria glared at him. 'What kept you?' She pushed past on to the landing.

'How do we stop them?' Rupam said. 'We've got about five minutes!'

'We have to get past *them* first,' Ben said.

One of the men was coming back up the stairs.

'Hide?' Rupam suggested. 'Back in the room and shut the door?'

Maria shook her head sadly. 'Boys,' she muttered, and strode purposefully along the landing.

She reached the top of the stairs at the same moment as the man did. He stopped, looking at her in surprise.

'Hi there,' Maria said brightly, smiling.

Then, bracing herself on one side with a hand on the banister rail and on the other with her shoulder against the wall, she lifted both feet off the floor and kicked out.

The blow caught the man full in the chest, knocking him down the stairs. He fell in a tangle of arms and legs, his cries lost in the increasing sound from the cellar. His head crashed against the wall, one foot tangled between banisters and he came to a halt, upside down. Silent and still.

'Don't just stand there gawping,' Maria said, her hands on her hips. 'We have to get Gemma. Come on.'

'Where are Knight and the others?' Rupam asked.

'Out cold. I left the door open for them.'

Maria had reached the bottom of the stairs and was waiting impatiently.

'I do think we need some sort of plan,' Rupam said. 'We can't just rush in and stop things.'

'Watch me,' Maria told him.

'Someone's coming,' Ben warned.

He could see a shadow in the doorway from the cellar. Maybe the other man had heard his friend stumble down the stairs, or perhaps he was coming to check on him . . .

'Hide and maybe he won't see us,' Rupam whispered.

For once, Maria didn't argue. They all pressed themselves into the shadowy recess of a doorway. They waited for agonising seconds as the man walked slowly past. Ben gave the others a thumbs-up. But he had forgotten the body of the first man.

The second man saw it at once, near the bottom of the stairs, and cried out in anger.

'I'll kill them for this!' His feet thumped up the stairs.

Ben felt the blood drain from his face. 'I'll stop him,' he heard himself say. 'You guys help Gemma.'

'Don't be daft,' Maria snapped. 'What can *you* do? You're about half his size. *I'll* stop him. You two get Gemma and stop Endeavour. I'll be right back.'

She ran after the man, following him rapidly and quietly up the stairs.

'Don't stand there gawping,' Rupam said, his hands on his hips in imitation of Maria. 'Come on. We've only got a couple of minutes!'

They had to struggle to get down the stone steps. It was like fighting their way along a wind tunnel. Ben had his hands in front of his face, trying to keep the stinging gale from his eyes.

As soon as they reached the bottom of the steps, they could see where the maelstrom of light and sound was coming from. The whole of the far side of the enormous cellar was a whirl of colour, spinning around a dark centre.

The cellar itself had a high, vaulted ceiling. It seemed to extend right under the house, the drive and gardens. The steps led down one side, bringing Ben and Rupam to the edge of a white circle painted on the dark stone floor. There were candles arranged round the edge of the circle and within the circle of flame was painted a red pentacle.

At the far end of the cellar, beneath the swirl

of colour and sound, stood Endeavour. He was wearing a dark gown now, the hood thrown back. In one hand he held a dagger. His other hand was clamped round Gemma's neck.

Rupam and Ben both shouted at the same moment. Ben rushed forward, but Rupam grabbed his arm.

'Don't cross into the circle.' He had to yell for Ben to hear him. 'Not good!'

There was a shape forming in the swirl of colour and sound. The blackness at its heart seemed to coalesce into something even darker. It grew and grew until it was blotting out the colour.

Endeavour turned, his face twisted in triumphant jubilation. He pulled Gemma closer, so that she was right in front of him. The wind and the noise slowly died away until there was almost silence.

'The calm before the storm.' Endeavour's voice echoed round the vaulted chamber. 'How kind of you both to join us for the final summoning of Mortagula.'

'We'll stop you!' Ben said, with more confidence than he felt.

Endeavour laughed. 'Oh, really? Others have tried. Just as they tried to stop Diablo. But I am greater even than he was. He needed the artefacts to focus his power. My will is stronger, my strength greater. I need no such toys and symbols. Mortagula is coming and you will witness my triumph.'

Ben started forward, determined to stop Endeavour. Even if it meant crossing into the circle. But a figure stepped in front of him. A figure holding a gun. Daniella Lawton.

'One final sacrifice, that's all it takes,' Endeavour said. He raised the dagger.

'No!' Rupam yelled. He started forward, but Daniella Lawton pushed him viciously away.

'Is that what you did to Sam?' Ben shouted. 'You murdered her? Sacrificed her? And for what? Nothing!'

'The final stage, to tame the demon,' Endeavour said. 'You knew Sam? She was the key that unlocked the gateway. Now I can open the doors of Hell itself with Gemma instead and allow Mortagula to enter our world.'

'You're mad!' Rupam shouted.

'I can control the demon, just as I control everything here.'

The cellar filled again with laughter.

But the laughter was deeper, louder, shaking the entire chamber. The darkness in the whirlpool of colour and light was a huge mouth filled with jagged teeth. The floor trembled under Ben's feet.

Endeavour had the dagger close to Gemma's throat. Ben could see the terror in her eyes, the pleading as she stared across at him and Rupam. But what could he do?

'*Effrego expositus libere!*' Endeavour exclaimed.

The cellar was once more filled with the sounds of wind and thunder. A finger of lightning stabbed out from the blackness at the heart of the storm. Endeavour was still speaking, but his words were sucked away into the elemental fury of Mortagula's arrival.

Ben and Rupam were having trouble staying on their feet. But so was Daniella Lawton. The storm was blowing round the cellar. Candles flickered and died.

'Mortagula arrives!' she shouted, triumphant.

But Ben was not so sure. 'Something's gone wrong!' he yelled.

On the other side of the circle, Endeavour was backing away. The low rumble of the creature's laughter again echoed round the chamber.

'He can't control it,' Rupam realised. 'He said he could do it without Diablo's artefacts – and he can't!'

Even as Rupam spoke, Endeavour was forced to his knees by the blast of power from the swirling darkness. Gemma seized her chance and tore free of his grasp. She scrambled away, careful to stay within the circle. Rupam had said to break the circle was dangerous and Gemma obviously knew that too.

Daniela Lawton looked on in horror and disbelief as the darkness closed in on Endeavour. She let the hand holding the gun dip away.

Without thinking, Ben kicked as hard as he could at her hand. She gave a cry of pain and rage, and the gun flew across the chamber. The moment it touched the circle of candles, it exploded into fiery fragments.

'We have to get Gemma out of there,' Rupam said.

'We have to stop the demon,' Ben yelled back. 'Once loose, it'll destroy everything.'

'But how?'

Endeavour was on his back, staring up at the massive dark claw emerging slowly from the air above him.

'You can do it,' Sam told Ben. 'Think! There has to be a way. You have to close the gateway before Mortagula comes through. You have to seal it tight shut!'

Seal it tight shut. Somewhere at the back of Ben's mind, the phrase was familiar. He'd heard it before. Rupam would know – he could remember everything. Except it wasn't something he'd heard when Rupam was there. He tried to replay it in his mind, tried to blot out the distractions:

Gemma cowering in the corner of the pentacle.

Endeavour desperately scrabbling away from the clawed arm that swiped down at him from the swirling gateway.

Daniella Lawton watching, hands to her face in undisguised horror.

Rupam yelling at Ben, 'What can we do?'

And suddenly Ben knew.

'That stuff he said, to open the gateway – it's the same as Knight says when he opens the Judgement Box.'

Rupam stared at him like he was mad.

'Don't you see? The words that Knight uses to seal the box *shut* – they might close the gateway.'

Rupam's mouth dropped open. 'That's brilliant. So – say the words!'

Now it was Ben's turn to gape. 'I don't know them – I've only heard him say them a couple of times.'

'We can close the gateway, but you don't know the words!'

'No, I don't.' Ben grabbed Rupam's shoulders, staring deep into his friend's eyes. 'But you do. You must have heard them.'

'That was years ago,' Rupam protested.

'It doesn't matter. You heard them once. And you remember everything. Absolutely everything!'

'Yes,' Rupam said quietly. 'Yes, I do.' He closed his eyes. 'I hope I do.'

'So do I,' Ben murmured.

The darkness had a shape. A second arm was reaching through the gateway into reality. The top of a shaggy horned head – darkness made manifest. Roars of triumph shook the building.

Rupam flung his arms out wide. '*Arceo excludum coerceo Hades terminus.*'

The change was abrupt and immediate. A mighty wind swept through the chamber. But it was not blowing from the gateway. It was rushing back into it. The force was so strong that Ben grabbed Rupam and together they struggled to stay on their feet.

Daniella Lawton was caught by surprise. Her feet were swept from under her and she was blown across the chamber. She rolled and tumbled, knocking aside candles as she was carried into the circle, struggling to grab hold of something. Her hands scrabbled in vain on the stone floor.

'The candles are out – the circle's broken,' Rupam was shouting. 'There's no protection any more. Gemma – you have to get out of there.'

Gemma hurled herself out of the pentacle. Caught in the middle, Endeavour was trying to crawl clear. The darkness was drawing back. The laughter had become roars of pain and anger. A final sudden gust of incredible power lifted Daniella Lawton off the ground – and hurled her into the centre of the darkness.

The whole of the cellar filled with a flare of red light.

Then there was silence.

Stillness.

Gemma pulled Rupam and Ben into a sobbing hug.

Sam watched from the shadows by the door, smiling. Over Gemma's shoulder, Ben smiled back.

Captain Morton and his men arrived just minutes later. They found a house filled with snuffed-out candles, laughing children and three adults with sore heads.

There were also three other people lying unconscious. One was in the alley beside the house. Another lay at the bottom of the main stairs. The third was lying half in and half out of a room with a steel door – just where Maria had left him.

But of Carstairs Endeavour – or his Grotesque – there was no sign.

'He'll try again,' Knight said.

They were all sitting on stools or the work surfaces in the kitchen while Morton's men checked the area round the house. Morton was in one of the other rooms, on the phone to the police to organise roadblocks and a helicopter search. But everyone knew that Endeavour was long gone.

'At least he failed,' Ben said. 'He couldn't control Mortagula – it almost killed him.'

'He needs all of Diablo's artefacts. He knows that now,' Growl said.

'And he's already got the dagger,' Rupam told them.

'Don't I know it,' Gemma said. 'It was made of Hellstorm metal all right.'

Maria put her arm protectively round the girl's shoulders. 'So what else is he after?'

'The two volumes,' Knight said. 'The amulet and the crystal. Then he'll try again, somewhere else.'

'A place of power, like this,' Madam Sosostram said. She was still looking pale and weak. 'We mustn't overlook how close he came to success.' She turned to Ben and Rupam. 'We owe our young colleagues a great debt of thanks.'

'Indeed we do,' Knight agreed. 'All of you. Well done. This war isn't over yet, but we've won the first battle.'

Captain Morton came back into the kitchen. 'Done what we can, but I'm not hopeful.'

'Have you searched the house?' Growl asked. 'I don't sense anything here, but it's as well to be sure.'

'We'll search it again. Nothing so far. Oh, except this . . .' He pulled a folded sheet of paper from his pocket and handed it to Knight.

Knight opened the paper. He stared at it for several moments without comment. Then he put it down on the kitchen table for everyone to see.

'What is it?' Rupam asked.

'It's a page from one of the volumes. From *The Book of Lost Souls*.'

'He has the book?' Madam Sosostram said.

Knight shook his head. 'This is a photocopy. The original page is quite safe. Or at least, I thought it was. I've not looked at it for years. I'd forgotten . . .' He glanced at Ben before going on: 'As I said, the war is just beginning, and the battles ahead may not be so easy.'

'You call that easy?' Rupam said. He nudged Ben. 'Easy – yeah, right.'

But Ben didn't respond. He was still looking at the photocopied page on the table. There was faint writing down one side, but most of the page was taken up with a picture – a drawing. It was a portrait of a girl.

'When was this book written?' he asked.

'In the seventeenth century,' Knight said quietly. 'It's one of Diablo's powerful volumes. But I think you recognise the girl in the picture, don't you? Which is more than I did a few weeks ago.'

Ben nodded. 'It's my sister,' he said.

Alone in his room at the School of Night, Ben sat on his bed and stared into space.

'Oh, Sam,' he murmured. 'I know what happened to you now. I don't understand much of it, but at least I *know*. You were never here, not really. And now I guess you're at peace.'

He drew in a deep, ragged breath, trying to hold back his tears. 'Endeavour's got away and we have to stop him. The world's so dangerous. There's so much going on. And I didn't know about any of it. And now I'm stuck here, on my own.'

'You don't get rid of me that easily,' Sam said.

Suddenly Sam was sitting beside him on the bed. She put her arm round her brother and held him tight as he cried quietly into her shoulder.

'We're in this together,' she told him. 'I promised.'